DATE DUE

Pearce, Michael
The Mamur Zapt and
the night of the dog

The Mamur Zapt
and the Night of the Dog

By Michael Pearce

THE MAMUR ZAPT AND THE NIGHT OF THE DOG
THE MAMUR ZAPT AND THE RETURN OF THE CARPET

MICHAEL PEARCE

The Mamur Zapt and the Night of the Dog

A Crime Club Book
DOUBLEDAY
New York London Toronto Sydney Auckland

A CRIME CLUB BOOK

PUBLISHED BY DOUBLEDAY
a division of Bantam Doubleday Dell Publishing Group, Inc.
666 Fifth Avenue, New York, New York 10103

DOUBLEDAY and the portrayal of a man
with a gun are trademarks of Doubleday,
a division of Bantam Doubleday Dell
Publishing Group, Inc.

All of the characters in this book are fictitious,
and any resemblance to actual persons, living or
dead, is purely coincidental.

Library of Congress Cataloging-in-Publication Data

Pearce, Michael, 1933–
The Mamur Zapt and the night of the dog / Michael Pearce. —1st ed.
in the U.S.A.
p. cm.
I. Title.
PR6066.E166M28 1991
823'.914—dc20 90-49973
CIP

ISBN 0-385-41521-4

Printed in the United States of America
May 1991
10 9 8 7 6 5 4 3 2 1
First Edition in the United States of America

The Mamur Zapt and the Night of the Dog

CHAPTER 1

The Mamur Zapt would have treated it all as a joke if Nikos, his official clerk, had not been so insistent.

"Get out there quick," he had said.

He had even volunteered to guide Owen to the Coptic Place of the Dead. Since Nikos was normally reluctant to take a single step outside his office, Owen had been impressed. Even so, if Georgiades had been around he might have sent him. Georgiades, however, was out on an errand of his own, or possibly still in bed. In any case, Nikos made it clear that he would not have approved.

"This is something for the Mamur Zapt," he said.

The Mamur Zapt was the head of Cairo's Political CID. Responsible in theory directly to Egypt's ruler, the Khedive, he answered in practice only to the British Consul-General, the man who, since Britain had charge of Egypt's purse strings, effectively controlled Egypt. The Consul-General, however, had taken pains not to define the Mamur Zapt's role too closely, observing that the less he knew of the Mamur Zapt's activities the more effective he was likely to be.

There were certain ground rules, however, and one of them was that the Mamur Zapt did not concern himself with routine police matters. Which he considered this to be.

"Police?" said Nikos, as if he could hardly believe his ears. "What good would they be?"

Owen had to admit there was something in this. The Cairo police force was recruited from country districts and consisted for the most part therefore of simple fellahin, or peasants, illiterate, underpaid and, when they got to the city, usually quite lost. Their duties tended to be restricted largely to the regulation of traffic, which, since the latter consisted chiefly of donkeys and camels, was in Nikos's view entirely appropriate. All real criminal investigation was left to the Parquet, the French-style Department of Prosecutions of the Ministry of Justice.

"The Parquet, then?" suggested Owen hopefully.

"The Mamur Zapt," said Nikos definitely, and put on his tarboosh and walked out of the door.

Owen put on his tarboosh too. Although he was still, strictly speaking, an army officer and merely on secondment, he considered himself now to be a civilian and preferred to dress in mufti. A tarboosh, the pot-like hat with a tassel which was the normal headgear of the educated Egyptian, was far less conspicuous than a sun helmet, especially of the heavy military sort. It was also cooler.

Not that that mattered too much this early in the morning. Later, when the sun was high in the sky and the temperature rose into the nineties, every little thing counted. Even the nature of your hat. At the moment, though, with the sun not long up over the horizon, the day was still pleasantly fresh and cool.

Owen borrowed a couple of constables from the orderly room at the front of the building and set out after Nikos.

They went on foot since their way lay through the mediaeval city, where the streets were too narrow and congested for a carriage to pass. This early in the morning the streets were not, in fact, very crowded. Almost the only people they saw were the black-gowned women drawing water for the day from the street pumps, but by the time they reached the Coptic Place of the Dead there were a lot more people around, and when Owen looked behind him he found that Nikos was not the only guide. From somewhere or other they had acquired a sizeable following of small boys and old men and others who might have been on their way to work if something more interesting had not come along.

Without assistance, although not necessarily on such a scale, Owen would never have found the house of Andrus, for it was set back from the ordinary thoroughfares of the necropolis and masked on all sides but one by huge family tombs. Once it came in sight, however, there was no mistaking it. A large crowd, mostly in the traditional dark gowns and dark turbans of the Copts, had already gathered around its front entrance. As Owen approached, the crowd parted and a man came up to him.

"This is an outrage!" the man said.

"An unfortunate incident, certainly," said Owen smoothly. Nikos had been able to brief him on the way.

"More than that," said the Copt, "much, much more than that."

"Don't let your distress—"

"They are trying to provoke us," the man cut in.

"They? Who?"

As soon as he had spoken, he could have cursed himself. For he knew what the answer would be.

"The Moslems," said the man. "The Moslems. They are behind this."

"Nonsense!"

It was important to stifle such ideas at birth. Cairo was an excitable city.

"Who else would have done it?"

"Children. Boys."

"Children!"

"Yes. For a joke."

"You call this a joke?"

"No. I say only that it is the sort of thing children would do as a joke."

"We know who did it," said someone in the crowd, "and it wasn't children."

"Nor was it a joke," said the man who had spoken first. "It was done to provoke us."

"So you say."

"So I know," the man retorted.

"How do you know?"

"This is not a thing in itself. It is part of a pattern."

"There have been other things?"

"Yes."

"What things?"

"Attacks on Copts in the streets. Women jostled on their way to church. Our priests spat on, children stoned."

"These are all bad things," said Owen, "but that is not enough to make a pattern."

"What more do you want?" asked the man. "Someone killed?"

"In a pattern," said Owen, "there is design."

"There is design here. Do you think these things happen by chance?"

"Women have always been jostled. Boys have always thrown stones."

"But not like this," said the man. "Our women dare not go out. We keep our children at home."

"There have been many such incidents?"

"Every day and increasingly."

"In one part of the city or in all?"

"At the moment," said the man, "in one part of the city only."

"And that is?"

"We are from the Mar Girgis," said the man. The Church of St. George, in the old part of the city, Owen thought. He had walked past it on his way to the cemetery.

"It is around there, is it?"

"Yes."

He became aware that the man was watching him closely.

"If you do not do something about it," the man said, "we shall."

The crowd went quiet. Owen suddenly noticed how much it had grown. It must be over two hundred. And with that realization came another. Not all of them were Copts.

"We have endured too much too long," the man said. "It is time to make an end of it."

"That is not for you," said Owen coldly. "It is for the Mamur Zapt."

This was ridiculous. To flare up over a thing as trivial as this! But he knew that was how things did catch fire in Cairo, and also that once started the fires were hard to put out.

"I will do something about it," he said.

"Do so!" said the man. "And do it quickly. For we will not wait."

The Mamur Zapt did not reckon to take this kind of talk from anyone, and he looked round for the police. But there were only two of them, huddled uneasily behind him. For the moment he could do nothing.

But he would have to do something. He couldn't leave the crowd like this. For the moment, the man seemed to have them in hand, but he could as easily incite as restrain. And if he did so, what would become of the Moslems present? There were only a few of them compared to the Copts. And what the hell were they doing here, anyway? You'd think they'd have enough sense to get out, fast.

He knew what they were doing. Watching the drama, like all Cairenes.

The thing to do was get this out of the public forum, get the drama off the streets.

He turned to the man who appeared to be the leader.

"There is no reason why you should wait," he said to him. "I am ready to hear what you have to say. Only not here. Can we go into the house?"

"Of course!" said the man.

He stepped aside and made a gesture of invitation.

"It is the house of Andrus," said Owen. "Where is Andrus?"

"I am Andrus," the man said.

The crowd opened and they walked through.

As he pushed past, someone in the crowd cried out. Owen looked up quickly but it was only an idiot, and he was a Copt, anyway. His head sagged to one side and his lips drooled. He called out again and this time Owen heard what he said.

"A death for a death!"

Owen turned in a flash, caught hold of him and threw him to one of the constables.

"Take him away, for Christ's sake," he said.

The constable's hands closed round the idiot as round a rabbit. As the boy was borne away he cried out once more: "A death for a death!"

"The boy is crazed," Owen said to those round about him. "To talk of such things when the only death in the affair is that of a dog!"

"So far," said Andrus.

Owen had hoped to disperse the crowd by going inside, but it didn't work. They followed him into the house. Cairenes had no sense of privacy, and they all wanted to know what was going to happen next. Owen was used to the publicness of Egyptian life and didn't really mind, especially now that the tension seemed to have eased, though he would have preferred fewer bodies in the room.

The room occupied the whole ground floor of the house. It wasn't a proper house but one used exclusively for visiting the dead. Coptic religious practice required attendance at the cemetery on specified nights of the year to remember and honour the dead, and many of the wealthier Copts kept "houses" in the cemetery just for that purpose. Like most such houses, this one consisted of two storeys, although the ground-floor room, a large room rather like a council chamber, was carried through in the middle of the house into the floor above. At this point a heavily ornamented balustrade ran round it creating a narrow promenade from which arches gave onto the apartments beyond. The upper floor was reserved for the women. As Owen made his way across the ground-floor room he was conscious of veiled, dark-gowned figures peeping down at him discreetly from behind the arches. The lower room had, as was common in well-to-do Egyptian houses, a sunken floor, at one end of which was a raised dais with leather cushions. This was where Owen was taken.

As he sat down, people pressed round him. A turbanned head craned intimately over his left shoulder, and as he slightly adjusted his position he found himself rubbing bristly cheeks with another head which was inserting itself on his right-hand side. The lower room was now so packed that people had opened the shutters in order to lean through the windows. All were entirely engrossed.

Andrus had sat down on the cushion opposite him. He was a thin, severe man in his late fifties with a gaunt face and prominent eye-sockets. His eyes looked very tired, which was not surprising if, as Owen supposed, he had spent the whole night at his prayers.

"Well, Andrus," he said, "let us begin. And let us begin with what happened last night. Speak to me as one who knows nothing."

"Very well."

Andrus paused to glance round the ring of onlookers, as if to make sure they were all attending.

"We came here to pass the night of the Eed el-Gheetas," he said, "as we usually do. You are aware of our custom, Captain Owen?"

Owen registered, as he was intended to, the correct use of his name and rank.

"We come here on feast days and also on some other occasions to honour our dead. I was especially anxious to come on this occasion as it is the anniversary of my father's death. He died four years ago. We spend the night in the house—"

"Not in the tomb?"

"Not in the tomb, no. We go there in the morning. First we have to prepare ourselves. We do that by keeping vigil."

"All through the night?"

"All through the night. We start at dusk."

"Did you go straight to the house? When you arrived, I mean? Or did you visit the tomb?"

"The others went to the house." There was a touch of disapproval in the words. "I went to the tomb."

"And you saw nothing untoward?"

"Not at the tomb, no."

"Or anywhere else?"

"There are always Moslems about in the necropolis nowadays," said Andrus coldly.

"But they weren't doing anything untoward?"

"No," said Andrus, with the air of one making a concession.

"How long did you stay at the tomb?"

"Not long. I paid my respects and then went on to the house."

"Where you stayed all night?"

"Yes."

"And again you saw and heard nothing untoward?"

"We were praying," said Andrus tartly.

"Of course. But you might have—"

"We did not."

Ordinarily, Owen would have probed but there was an impatient finality about the words. He moved Andrus on.

"Then in the morning—?"

"We went to the tomb."

"Where you found—?"

Andrus made a gesture of disgust as if he could hardly bring himself to speak of it.

"Where you found—?" Owen prompted again.

"A dog!" Andrus spat out. "At the very door of my father's tomb!"

He glared round dramatically. Totally involved, the crowd gave a sympathetic gasp.

"I feel for you," said Owen tactfully. "I feel for you. But . . ." He hesitated and chose his words with care. "Is there not a possibility—I ask only to make sure—that the dog came there by accident?"

"Accident?" said Andrus incredulously.

"There are lots of dogs in the cemetery," said Owen, "and some of them are old and sick. Might not one of them, knowing that its time to die had come—"

"Have dragged itself across the graveyard until by chance it arrived at my father's tomb?"

"Yes."

"—and then, with its last breath, climbed up a flight of six steep steps and forced open the heavy door that was barred against it? Pah."

Andrus made a gesture of derision. The crowd laughed scornfully.

"First, it was a joke. Now it is a fairy tale."

Owen went patiently on.

"The door was barred?"

"Yes."

"Not locked?"

"I unlocked it the night before when I came first to the tomb."

"But left it barred? Are you sure?"

"Surer of that," said Andrus, with a sidelong glance at the crowd, "than that the dog lifted the bar itself."

The crowd laughed with him.

"The point is important," Owen insisted. "If the door were open, the dog could have come there itself."

"It was brought," said Andrus, "by other dogs. Moslem ones."

"Where did you find the dog? Inside the tomb?"

"In the doorway. Half inside, half out."

"And dead?"

"Quite dead," said Andrus.

"You say it was Moslems."

"I know it was Moslems."

"Did anyone see them?"

Andrus hesitated. "No one has said so."

"I will ask. And I will ask more widely. It may be that someone saw them bring the dog into the cemetery."

"There are dogs in the cemetery enough."

Owen shrugged. "I will check, anyway. I will also ask those in your house."

"I speak for them."

"It may be that one of them heard something or saw something that you did not."

Now it was Andrus who shrugged his shoulders.

"It may be that no one saw anything or heard anything. They came like thieves in the night."

"It is important, however, to check. Then we might establish whether it was indeed Moslems."

"Who else could it have been?"

"Copts. Have you any enemies?"

"Only Moslems," said Andrus.

He seemed stuck on this. Owen could not tell whether it was some personal bitterness or whether it was the general bitterness which he knew Copts felt for Moslems. If it was the latter, he was surprised at its intensity. If that was widely shared, then it was worrying. There was the possibility of a major explosion. And any little spark could set it going.

Even the death of a dog.

He understood now why Nikos had been so insistent that he come.

"And what the hell were you doing while all this was going on?" asked Georgiades.

"I am in the office," Nikos said with dignity. "I leave the other stuff to you."

He paused impressively, looked through the sheaf of papers he was holding in his hand, pulled one out and laid it on the desk in front of Owen.

"All I can find out about Andrus," he said.

Owen glanced at it, but then looked back at Nikos.

"Tell me," he said. It would be sensible for Georgiades to hear.

"A zealot," said Nikos.

"Extremist?"

"Not in your sense, no," said Nikos coldly. He was himself a Copt. "Just very religious. You would consider excessively so."

Nikos liked to get things exactly right.

"But not politically active?"

"No known Nationalist connections, if that's what you're asking."

"I wasn't. Not specifically. I was wondering if he was active in politics generally?"

"How can a Copt be active in politics generally?"

The Copts, although the direct descendants of the Egyptians of the pharaohs, were now in a minority in Egypt. They numbered less than a million. There were over eight million Moslems. Since before the days of the Mamelukes Egypt had been a Moslem country. Successive sultans, and the generals who had governed Egypt for them, had not even thought of sharing their rule with the Copts, nor had more recent khedives seen any reason to depart from that tradition. Even the new Western-style political parties which were springing up had restricted Coptic participation.

"You know what I mean," said Owen. "Behind the scenes."

But although Copts had been effectively excluded from direct participation in government they participated indirectly in very considerable measure. They were prominent in the civil service. Indeed, you could almost say that the civil service was run by them. Even in what was called in other countries parliamentary politics they were not without influence. They were energetic and skilful lobbyists. One thing they were not, thought Owen, was inactive in politics.

"I know what you mean." Nikos caved in, having made his point. "No, he is not. He confines his public activities to church work, of which he does a lot."

"The Mar Girgis?"

"Yes. That's right."

"What sort of church is it?"

"Fundamentalist. Conservative. Ascetic."

"That figures."

"Yes," said Nikos, "he's like that, too."

"Anything else?"

"A prominent figure in the local Coptic community. Name any committee and he's on it. Any list of subscriptions and he's at the top."

"Where does he get the money?"

"He's a businessman. Soft fruit, raisins, grapes, that sort of thing. He imports them and exports them. His main place of business is really Alexandria, though he prefers to live in Cairo himself, which is where his family have always lived and where his father built up the family business."

"His father is dead?"

"Yes. He'd been in ailing health for some years. He suffered badly in one of the massacres."

"Massacres?"

"Of the Copts. By the Moslems."

"I see."

"Yes," said Nikos, "I thought you would."

Among the papers which Nikos had brought in were the office accounts. These made gloomy reading. They were still some weeks from the end of the financial year and already Owen was almost spent up. He decided he would have to see Garvin about it. Garvin was the Commandant of the Cairo Police and although not formally Owen's superior was the man he in practice reported to. Garvin had very good links with the Consul-General.

He was also the person in whose budget, for administrative convenience, Owen's accounts were included, so any application for an increase would have to be cleared with him.

Owen was not expecting any difficulty. The Mamur Zapt's budget was relatively small and the work important. Since Cromer's time, however, the Ministry of Finance had been sticklers for financial probity and formal permission would definitely have to be obtained. The British Consul-General had been brought in specifically to clear up the Egyptian financial mess and by the time he had left, two years ago, the Government's accounts had been transformed. Some were saying, the new English Liberal MPs among them, that Britain's work in Egypt was now completed and that there was no excuse for them staying further. It had, after all, been thirty years.

Before going to Garvin, however, Owen was anxious to

check the accounts. A previous Mamur Zapt had been dismissed for corruption not so long previously that Owen could afford to ignore criticism. He was deep in calculations when the phone rang.

It was one of the Consul-General's aides, a personal friend of his.

"Hello," said Paul, "I was trying to get you earlier but you were out. I need some help."

"Yes?"

"Visitors. Important ones. Ones who need special handling."

"So?"

"I at once thought of you."

"No," said Owen. "Definitely not. Much too busy. Quite out of the question. No."

"It is not I alone who thinks so. The Consul-General thinks so too."

"You put the idea in his head."

"We reviewed the possibilities together. I may have suggested there was a need for some dexterity. Political dexterity."

"You rotten sod."

"I have your interests at heart. Also my own. We don't want this to go wrong."

"I'm sorry. I've got more important things to do."

"You haven't. This has priority. So says the Consul-General."

"Bloody hell! I've got a lot on just now."

"Then put a lot off."

"Who the hell are these visitors?"

"You only need to bother about one of them. Well, let's say one and a half. He has a niece with him. He, John Postlethwaite, is one of the new intake of Liberal MPs and has chosen to make a speciality of Egypt. This is because none of the other committees would have him. Retrenchment, reform and Bolton's backyard is all he really knows about. Oh, and accounts. He took Cromer to task over his and made something of a name for himself. That's what gave him the idea. Of specializing in Egypt, I mean. He wants to come out and see things at first hand. The accounts, that is."

"McPhee sounds just the man for this," said Owen, selling the Assistant Commandant down the river without a qualm.

"McPhee? Not in a million years. This is out of his class. This is a delicate exercise, boyo, and not for the McPhees of this world. Haven't you been listening? We need someone with some political sense. This is important, I keep telling you. There's a lot at stake. My job for a start. Yours too, probably. It's not trivial stuff like The End of Empire, Egypt's Manifest Destiny, or England's Moral Mission to Confuse the World. Christ, did I say that? I'm going to have to watch my step for the next two months."

"Two months? For Christ's sake, I can't spend that amount of time."

"You can do other things as well," said Paul magnanimously.

"I'm afraid so," said Garvin.

"But it's going to take up hours," Owen complained. "Just when I'm especially busy."

"What are you busy on?"

Owen told him about the dog. Garvin, knowledgeable in the ways of Egypt, took it seriously.

"Christ!" he said. "If you don't sort that out quickly they'll be at each other's throats."

"So I can concentrate on that and get someone else to look after Postlethwaite?"

"You can concentrate on that and still look after Postlethwaite. Don't spend too much time on him, that's all."

As Owen went out, Garvin said: "You'd better get it sorted out by the twenty-fifth."

"Why?"

"That's the Coptic Easter Monday. It's also the day when the Moslems have a Moulid for some local saint or other. I think they do it just to be awkward. The problem is to keep the processions apart, because of course if they run into each other there's all kinds of trouble, especially if things are a bit tense between them anyway. But that's not till the twenty-fifth. You'll have it all sorted out by then. I hope."

CHAPTER 2

In deference to the susceptibilities of Moslem guests, the reception took the form of an English tea. The setting was appropriate. Once guests had been received and presented to the Consul-General's wife, they passed out onto the beautiful Residency lawns. There, among the herbaceous borders, the great coloured splashes of bignonia, bougainvillaea and clerodendrons, the rose-gardens and the citrus grove, they were served with tiny cucumber sandwiches and cups of tea by immaculate white-turbanned waiters. No alcohol was served, and the red-faced, heavy-jowled senior army officers had to grit their teeth and wait for the hour of their release.

The arrangement suited the Member of Parliament for Warrington since he was a Nonconformist, a teetotaller and a Liberal, all three of which characteristics he assumed, correctly, to be rare in army officers, especially in Egypt, which he seemed to confuse with the land of Sodom and Gomorrah. He kept a stern eye open for evidence of possible depravity in any young officer who approached his niece and Owen was glad that he had decided to appear at the reception in mufti.

It also helped that Owen was Welsh. Wales was, of course, a stronghold of Liberalism and Nonconformity and, slightly uneasy among all this exoticism, John Postlethwaite fell back on the things he was familiar with, which included, he thought, Owen.

"I'll want to see everything, mind," he warned Owen. "No pulling the wool over my eyes."

"I'll want to see everything too, Captain Owen," his niece said, "although, of course, they may not be the same things."

"The accounts," said John Postlethwaite.

"Egypt," said his niece.

So far, Owen had not been able to make out Miss Postlethwaite. For one thing, he couldn't see her, since she had disappeared almost entirely under a huge sunbonnet. She had none of the racy, quasi-emancipated slang of the other girls and he might have taken her altogether for a shrinking Nonconformist violet had he not once caught a very sharp eye appraising him carefully from under the bonnet.

"We might even be able to make a start on the accounts now," he said, and led them over to an Egyptian he knew slightly who worked in the Ministry of Finance. The Egyptian took in the politics of the situation in a flash and moved smoothly into diplomatic conversation with the MP. Within seconds both were deep in technical matters.

"That's the accounts taken care of," said Jane Postlethwaite. "What about me?"

"What would you like to see?"

"Cairo," said Jane. "You can start this evening."

Mr. Postlethwaite looked up uneasily.

"We already have an engagement for this evening, my dear," he protested.

"That is not an engagement," said Jane. "It is merely something laid on by the hotel."

"Nevertheless—"

"You can go to that, Uncle John. I shall be quite safe with Captain Owen."

Both uncle and niece were captured shortly afterwards by the Consul-General's wife and Owen was left alone for a moment with the Egyptian.

"What are you busy with just now?" asked Ramses Bey, who knew what Owen's work was.

"Copts and Moslems."

"As usual," said Ramses, who was himself a Copt.

"Is it as usual?" asked Owen.

Ramses gave him a sideways glance.

"Well," he said, "that's an interesting question."

"I was hoping you were going to tell me if there was anything that might be making it unusual."

"I don't think I shall be telling you anything," said Ramses.

He stretched out a hand for a passing cucumber sandwich. The waiter lifted the tray towards him. Between them a sandwich fell to the ground. Before either could move, a dark shape darted between them, scooped up the sandwich and flew off to the far end of the garden where McPhee, the Assistant Commandant, was locked in conversation with a rather intense Egyptian.

"These damned hawks," said Ramses. He caught sight of McPhee.

"Shall we rescue your colleague?" he suggested. "He looks as if he might need it."

McPhee glanced up with relief as they approached.

"Just the man!" he said to Owen. "Sesostris Bey feels that not enough is being done to protect the Coptic community. Have you met? Captain Cadwallader—"

Owen winced. He tried to keep his middle name hidden under a bushel.

"—Owen," McPhee concluded with relish. He had a soft spot for legendary Celtic names, however dubious the descendancy. "The Mamur Zapt."

"The Mamur Zapt?" Sesostris looked at Owen sharply. "Yes, indeed."

Both Copts were small, spare men and both wore modern European suits; but whereas Ramses dressed with elegance and even a touch of dash, Sesostris wore his with severe Coptic sobriety.

"Why do you feel that not enough is being done to protect the Coptic community?" asked Owen.

There was no hesitation about Sesostris. He plunged at once into a catalogue of grievances, wrongs which the Moslems had allegedly committed against the Copts. Most of them were trivial. A shop had been broken into here, stones thrown there. People had been jostled in the market or spat on on their way to church. A few incidents were more serious. Solitary individuals had been set upon by gangs of Moslem youths and beaten up. A prayer meeting had been disrupted. Owen made a mental note to check up on these. The list culminated, as he had half-expected it would, with the business about the dog.

"Ah! The dog! Yes," he murmured. Over Sesostris's shoulder he saw Ramses cock a quizzical eye.

"It is no light matter," said Sesostris sharply. "We will not allow our dead to be insulted."

"There may have been no insult," said Owen.

"Ah yes," said Sesostris. "I have heard of your theory."

"I have no theory yet. I am merely checking possibilities."

"Do not check too long," said Sesostris.

Ramses placed a restraining hand on Sesostris's sleeve.

"Surely Captain Owen is right to check," he protested. "There has been far too much precipitate action between Copt and Moslem."

"You would naturally think so."

"Why would Ramses Bey naturally think so?" asked Owen.

"Because he has taken sides."

"I work for the Government, if that's what you mean."

"Copts have always worked for the Government," said Owen. "With their industry and talent it is a natural thing to do."

"Whoever governs Egypt, we do," said Ramses.

"No, you don't!" said Sesostris, turning on him. "You merely think you do. It is our big mistake. By working with the Government we support it. We should work against it."

"Should you?" asked Owen.

"Yes," said Sesostris fiercely. "I know what you think, Captain Owen. You want what the British want. Power, and a quiet life. It is what every conqueror of Egypt has wanted. For two thousand years we Copts have worked with every government. And for two thousand years every government has been that of an invader. Perhaps it is time we changed our tactics."

"Enjoy what you have," said Owen, "or you might lose it."

Sesostris smiled wintrily.

"Threaten the Moslems, Captain Owen, not me. Or your life may not be quiet."

He walked off.

McPhee spluttered indignantly.

"Nasty fellow," he said. Then he caught Ramses's eye, went red in the face and began to apologize profusely.

Ramses laughed and patted McPhee's arm.

"Don't worry," he said. "You're not the only one who finds him difficult."

The three of them walked back slowly to the centre of the lawn where the majority of the guests had congregated. A little knot had gathered around the Consul-General. Most of them were ministers. One of them, recently appointed in a reshuffle by the Khedive, and known to Owen, greeted him as he came up. Owen returned the greeting.

"And how is your son getting on, Nuri Pasha?" he asked.

The son was in France; for the benefit of his health.

Nuri Pasha raised eyes heavenwards. "At least he's a long way away," he said.

"And how is my daughter, Captain Owen?" he asked in return.

Jane Postlethwaite, standing nearby, turned her face slightly under her sunbonnet.

"Quite well, thank you, sir," Owen replied. "I rather expected she would be here."

He scanned the crowd but Zeinab was nowhere to be seen.

"She has a mind of her own," said Nuri. "Fortunately."

He was pulled back into the inner circle.

"He might not be here for long," said Ramses. "The word is that another reshuffle is on the cards."

A man detached himself from the circle and made his way familiarly into the Residency.

"That could be the man to watch," said Ramses. "He has done very well in our ministry. The Consul-General likes him."

"Who is he?"

"Patros Bey."

A Copt.

McPhee had told Owen that there was a gathering of the Zikr that night so he thought he would take Miss Postlethwaite to it to show her some local colour.

"The Zikr are a sort of sect, Miss Postlethwaite," he explained. "Moslem, of course. The name refers to their practice of repeating the name of God, Allah, innumerable times."

"It sounds very interesting," said Miss Postlethwaite doubtfully.

Owen laughed.

"That's not all there is to it. They whirl and dance and eat fire and that sort of thing. Sometimes they stick knives in themselves. In fact, they used to carry things to such an extreme that a few years ago the Government was obliged to step in and ban the most excessive practices."

"Did they accept the ban?"

"More or less. You see, it was done with the support of their Grand Mufti—the religious leader so far as ecclesiastical law is concerned—who thought that the whole thing had become too self-indulgent."

"Sticking knives in themselves is self-indulgent?"

"In theological terms, yes, apparently."

Miss Postlethwaite was silent for some time. Then she asked: "Are you a theologian, Captain Owen?"

"I will introduce you to my colleague, Mr. McPhee, the Assistant Commandant of the Cairo Police, who has a great interest in local theology and religious customs. However," said Owen, who did not feel that this line was particularly promising, "there will also be snake-charmers, acrobats, jugglers, that sort of thing, which I hope you will find equally interesting."

Well before they reached the place where the Zikr were assembled they heard the sound of drumming and tambourines and as they came into the square they saw that the Zikr had already begun their chanting. There were about thirty of them, sitting cross-legged upon matting in the centre of the square, forming a kind of oblong ring. In the middle of the ring were three very large wax candles, each about four feet high and stuck in a low candlestick. In their light the Zikr could be seen clearly, staring at the flames, swinging their heads and bodies in time to the music, and chanting repeatedly *"La ilaha illa Allah*—there is no god but God."

As these were still in the nature of "warming up" exercises, the crowd took no great interest, concentrating instead on the ancillary services inseparable from any public occasion in Cairo. They clustered round the tea stalls, coffee stalls, sherbet stalls and sweetmeat stalls and sampled the chestnuts from the braziers at the foot of the trees. They watched with only an apparent lack of interest the tumblers, jugglers, snake-charmers, baboon-walkers, flute-players and story-tellers competing to entertain them. And they were lured in surprising numbers to the dark edges of the square, where veiled women from the villages read their fortune in the sand.

Owen took to all this like a Cairene; not so much the goods or turns in themselves as the pretext they provided for backchat and bonhomie. He had long ago come to the conclusion that the chief business of the Egyptian was conversation and that Egyptian institutions should be judged by the contribution they made to that. By that criterion the stall-holders, street-vendors and performers rated high. Round every stall was a knot of people all arguing vigorously. Owen would have liked to have joined in and normally would have done so. However, he felt slightly constrained by Miss Postlethwaite's presence. He wondered, indeed, as he piloted her round the various turns in the open parts of the square, whether she was enjoying herself.

Once, she gave a little jump. This was when a baboon belonging to one of the street-performers put its hand in hers. Owen gave it the necessary milliemes and it released her hand and scuttled back to its owner.

"Don't be alarmed, Miss Postlethwaite," he said reassuringly. "They're quite harmless. They look rather unpleasant, I know, especially when they're exploited like this. But they're the very same creatures as appear in the paintings in the tombs."

It sounded horribly like the patter of the dragomans as they showed tourists round the Pyramids.

"Really?" said Miss Postlethwaite, slightly distantly.

She revived a little when they left the turns behind them and began to thread their way through the stalls. As always with a Cairo crowd, there was immense ethnic variety, and her interest seemed genuine as Owen pointed out the different types: the Nubians from the south, with their darker skins and scarred cheeks; the Arish from the Eastern Desert, the hawk-faced men with silver-corded headcloths and striped burnooses, their women unveiled but with their feet covered, as opposed to the ordinary Cairo women who exposed their legs but kept their faces concealed. He drew her attention to the dark turbans of the Copts. Was it his imagination or were there rather a lot of them? This was, after all, a Moslem occasion. He was beginning to think he had Copts on the brain when he heard one or two of the sweetmeat-sellers calling out, "A grain of salt in the eye of him who does not bless the Prophet," the traditional cry for warding off bad luck, and knew he was not mistaken.

He bought Miss Postlethwaite a sherbet at one of the stalls and asked the stall-keeper why there were so many Copts around.

"Didn't you know?" the man said. "This is the Moulid of Sheikh Darwish el-Ashmawi. All the expenses are paid by a

Copt who became a Moslem." He grinned. "They don't like to see their money go so they come and eat it up."

"To your great benefit, no doubt."

The man mopped up a spill on the counter.

"I wish the benefit was greater," he said.

"What is a Moulid?" Jane Postlethwaite asked.

"It's a sort of feast-day for the local saint. In Egypt there are lots and lots of saints. Every village has one. Most have several. There are feast-days all the time. Everyone has a lot of fun."

"Saints," said Jane Postlethwaite, "and baboons!"

A change in the tempo of the drumming drew their attention back to the Zikr.

"The party's starting," said Owen, standing up. "It's time for us to go."

To one side of the Zikr was a roped-off enclosure for the elderly and more decorous. In it they were given cushions and coffee and settled back to watch developments. They were not long in coming.

In their absence the chanting had become more complex. Now it was more like an English catch-song or round. One group of Zikr would take up a phrase, embroider it and then give it to the others. In turn they would repeat it, embroider and give it back again. Gradually, the process became faster and faster until there was hardly a gap between the giving of a phrase and receiving it back again and all the Zikr seemed to be shouting all the time. The music rose to a crescendo.

Suddenly, one of the Zikr leaped into the middle of the ring and began to utter loud gasps in time with the words of the others. More and more of the Zikr joined in until they were all on their feet gasping in unison.

The gasping quickened. Someone else sprang into the centre of the ring and began to spin like a top, the skirt of his gown flying out around him like a huge umbrella. Other Zikr started to jump up and down and some of them rushed round the ring contorting their bodies and making little stabbing motions with their hands. All of them were screaming. The music rose to new heights. The uproar was terrific.

The man swirling in the centre stopped and stepped out of the ring. For a moment the music faltered. Then there was a piercing scream and another man sprang into the centre. He was very tall and black, a Nubian of some sort, and at once he began to leap up and down, holding his arms up so that his hands were locked above his head, all the time screaming "Allah! Allah! Allah!" He went on like this for several moments and then collapsed foaming on the ground. Two of the Zikr carried him aside.

The music faltered again and then began to pound even more insistently. Another Zikr sprang forward. This one kept bounding into the air, beating his breast and calling out, until suddenly he rushed to one side, picked up a short Sudanese stabbing spear and plunged it into his body. It seemed to have no effect. He did it again with another spear and then another. In a moment he seemed to be bristling with them.

Another Zikr began calling out for fire. Someone brought him a small copper chafing-dish full of red-hot charcoal. He seized a piece of charcoal and put it in his mouth. He did the same with another and another until his mouth was full, and then he deliberately chewed the live coals, opening his mouth wide every few moments to show its contents. When he inhaled, the coals glowed almost to white heat; and when he exhaled, sparks flew out of his mouth.

Someone brought a thorn bush into the ring and set it alight. One of the Zikr took it and thrust it up inside his robe, all the time continuing with his dancing. As he whirled round, his robe billowed out and the flames blazed up, so that his gown seemed full of fire. There was the great blaze in the darkness and above it the exalted, ecstatic face looking up to heaven.

Everywhere, now, was fire. And everywhere, too, men were rushing around with daggers and spears sticking in their throats, cheeks, mouths, faces, stomachs and chests. They danced and whirled and cried "Allah" continuously. The drums beat on, the flutes shrilled, and the music swirled to new heights of passion. All over the square now people were dancing and jumping.

Beside Owen, an elderly man sprang to his feet, tore off most of his clothes, and leaped into the circle. In a moment he was jumping skyward, his face contorted, his chest heaving with great gasps of "Allah."

The Zikr danced on and on. They did not seem to tire, nor

did they seem affected by the stabbing or the fire. After whirling for perhaps five or ten minutes they would stop and step out of the ring for a moment, apparently steady and completely free from giddiness. They would pause only for an instant and then rejoin the ring.

Towards midnight the music slackened. No new coals were brought, and as the flames died out, the Zikr quietened. Their dance became a steady rhythmic leaping. Their voices, hoarse now, could manage only a rapt murmur of "Allah." One by one they fell out of the dance and collapsed to the ground, until there were only two or three whirling in the middle. Eventually, their spinning, too, came to an end.

The music stopped.

A great sigh rose from the onlookers like a collective release. It was as if a spell had been broken. They sat back and as it were rubbed their eyes.

For a moment or two there was silence. And then one or two people began to talk, quietly at first but then more animatedly, and soon normal babble was resumed.

A white-bearded Zikr attendant came round with coffee and then, noting Miss Postlethwaite, returned with almond cakes.

"We should eat them," said Owen, uneasily aware of the hour and thinking about Mr. Postlethwaite back in the hotel. "It is wrong to refuse hospitality."

"I would not dream of doing so," said Jane Postlethwaite, and tucked in with relish. "It is not, of course, the kind of religious occasion that I am used to but it was most interesting."

Owen was relieved. It was some time since he had been to a Zikr gathering and he had forgotten what strong meat it was.

A Zikr walked past him. Owen recognized him as the one who had put the blazing thorn bush inside his gown. He was dressed now only in a loin-cloth—the gown had burnt. Owen looked at him closely. There were no traces on his skin either of burns or of thorn scratch marks. He looked over to where some of the other Zikr were standing. These were ones who had stabbed themselves with spears and swords and one or two of them still had knives sticking in them. They looked very, very tired but not hurt. There was a thin trickle of blood coming from some of the wounds. It was nothing like the mutilations, however, which some of the sects practised. These were often combined with self-flagellation and then there was blood everywhere. In the case of the Zikr the intention was not to humiliate but to exalt, to demonstrate the imperviousness of the body when it is caught up in Allah's holy rapture.

Gradually all the Zikr who had collapsed to the ground rose to their feet. Except one, who as the minutes went by remained still.

CHAPTER 3

Paul was cross.

"I said show her the sights," he complained. "I didn't mean that sort of sight."

"How was I to know it would end like that?"

"Well, Christ, if they're always sticking knives in themselves, one day it was bound to happen. Anyway, is that the sort of thing you take a girl to? People sticking knives in themselves? Jesus, Gareth, you've got funny ideas of entertainment. You were out on that goddamn Frontier a bit too long."

"She wanted to go," Owen protested.

"She didn't know what the hell she wanted. You should have had more sense. Couldn't you have taken her to a mosque or something? She's religious, isn't she?"

"She wanted to see a bit of Cairo life."

"Cairo life, yes, but not Cairo death. Honestly, Gareth, I'm disappointed in you. Where the hell's your judgement?"

Garvin was even crosser.

"The Consul-General has been on to me," he said, "personally. He wants to know, and I want to know too, what the bloody hell you were doing. You're not some wet-behind-the-ears young subaltern fresh out from England without a bloody idea in his head. You're the Mamur Zapt and ought to have some bloody political savvy."

"She wanted to see Cairo—"

"Then show her Cairo. Show her the bloody Pyramids or something. Take her down the Musky and let her buy something. Take her to the bazaars. Take her to the Market of the Afternoon. Take her to the bloody Citadel. But don't bloody take her somewhere where she's going to see somebody get his throat cut."

"He didn't actually—"

Garvin paused in his tirade. "Yes," he said, in quite a different voice, "that was a bit odd, wasn't it? They usually know what they're doing. However"—his voice resumed its previous note—"the one thing you're supposed to be doing is handling this pair with kid gloves. Taking this girl to a Zikr gathering is not that."

He glared at Owen, defying him to defy him. Owen had enough political sense at least not to do that.

"And that's another thing," said Garvin. "You were supposed to be showing them both around. Both. Not just the girl. This is not a personal Sports Afternoon for you, Owen, it's bloody work. This man is important. With the new Government in England, these damned MPs are breathing down our necks. They're on our backs already. This visit was a chance to get them off our backs. The Consul-General wants to build bridges. Any bloody bridge he wanted to build," said Garvin pitilessly, "is shattered and at the bottom of the ravine right now. Thanks to you. Postlethwaite is going crazy. He's demanding apologies all round. The Consul-General's apologized, I've apologized—"

"I certainly apologize," said Owen stiffly.

"You do?" said Garvin with heavy irony. "Oh, good of you. Most kind."

"I shall see it doesn't happen again."

"You won't get the bloody chance," said Garvin.

Back at the office there were soon developments. They were not, however, of the sort that Owen had expected.

"Visitors," said Nikos.

Owen rose to greet them. There were three. Two of them were religious sheikhs and the third was an assistant kadi. There was a separate judicial system in Egypt for Mohammedan law presided over by a separate chief judge, the kadi. It was the assistant kadi who spoke first.

"We have come to lay a complaint," he said.

"A complaint? In what connection?"

"It concerns a killing. It happened last night. We understand that you were there."

"A Zikr? At the gathering? If so, I was there."

The assistant kadi looked at the two sheikhs. They appeared pleased.

"He was there, you see," one of them said.

"Then he will know," said the other.

"What should I know, Father?" asked Owen courteously.

"How it came about."

"I expect you are already working on it," said the assistant kadi.

"On what?" asked Owen, baffled.

"On the murder."

"Murder? I saw no murder."

"But you were there," said one of the sheikhs, puzzled.

"A man died. I saw that."

"But it was murder. It must have been. A Zikr would not die as he was reaching towards his God."

"Allah takes people at any time," said Owen as gently as he could.

The sheikh shook his head.

"I know what you are thinking," he said. "It wasn't like that."

"What am I thinking?" asked Owen.

"You are thinking he died from his own hand."

"Well—"

"It was not like that. A Zikr knows."

"Knows where to put the knife? Yes, but in the—" Owen hesitated; the word "frenzy" was on the tip of his tongue—"moment of exaltation" he substituted. "In the moment of exaltation who knows what may have happened?"

The sheikh shook his head firmly.

"Allah guides his hand," he said with certainty.

"The Zikr does not make mistakes," said the other sheikh, with equal conviction.

They met Owen's gaze with a simple confidence which Owen felt it would be churlish to challenge.

"If he did not die by his own hand," said Owen slowly, "then how did he die?"

"By the hand of another."

Owen paused deliberately.

"Such things should not be said lightly."

The sheikhs agreed at once.

"True."

"He speaks with justice."

"Then how"—Owen paused—"can you be sure?"

The sheikhs looked a little bewildered.

"The Zikr do not make mistakes. Allah guides their hand," they explained again, patiently, rather as if they were speaking to a child.

Owen normally had no difficulty in adjusting to the slow tempo and frequent circularity of Arab witnesses but this morning, what with the events of the last two days, he felt his patience under strain.

"There must be further grounds," he said.

The sheikhs looked at each other, plainly puzzled.

"The Zikr do not—" one began.

The assistant kadi intervened with practised authority.

"There was talk of a man."

"During the dance?"

"During the dance."

"Just talk?"

"There are others who claim to have seen."

"What sort of man?"

He could have guessed.

"A Copt," the two sheikhs said in unison.

As the three left, Owen detained the assistant kadi for a moment.

"The Parquet's been informed, I take it?"

"Yes. However, as you were there—"

"Yes, indeed. Thank you."

"Besides"—the assistant kadi glanced at the retreating backs of the sheikhs—"there could be trouble between the Moslems and the Copts. I shouldn't be saying it, I suppose, but I thought you ought to be involved."

"I'm grateful. It is important to hear of these things early."

"You'll have no trouble with these two," the assistant kadi went on confidentially, "nor with the people in the Ashmawi mosque. It's the sheikh in the next district you'll have to watch out for. He's jealous of all the money going to the Ashmawi. Besides, he hates the Copts like poison."

Owen rang up his friend in the Parquet.

"Hello," said Mahmoud.

"There's a case just come up. A Zikr killing. A Zikr death, anyway," he amended. "Do you know who's on it?"

"Yes," said Mahmoud. "Me."

"Thank Christ for that," said Owen.

"Have you an interest?"

"You bet I have. Can we have a talk about it?"

"About half an hour? The usual place?"

They met on neutral ground, that is to say a café equidistant between the Parquet offices and the Bab el-Khalkh, where Owen worked. Relations between the departments were at best lukewarm and there were also practical advantages in confidentiality. Sometimes the right hand got further if it did not know what the left hand was doing. Also, although Owen had known Mahmoud for about a year now and they were good friends, their relationship was—perhaps necessarily—sometimes an uneasy one. Owen was more senior and had an access to power which Mahmoud would never have. Besides which, there were all the usual tensions between Egyptian and Englishman (or, in Owen's case, Welshman), Imperialist and Nationalist, occupier and occupied. At times, too, Owen found Mahmoud's emotional volatility difficult to handle; and no doubt Mahmoud on his side found British stolidity just as exasperating. There was an element of emotional negotiation in their relationship which was best managed away from their own institutions. If the meeting had been at the Ministry of Justice or at Police Headquarters both would have had to play roles. Sitting outside the café in this narrow back street, with only the occasional forage-camel plodding past with its load of berseem, they could talk more freely.

"I've only just received the case. You were there, I gather?"

"Yes."

"With this Miss Postlethwaite." Mahmoud stumbled slightly over the word. Although he spoke English well, he spoke French better, and the word came out sounding as it would have done if a Frenchman had pronounced it.

"Yes. She's the niece of an MP who's visiting us. Got to be looked after. You won't want to see her, will you?"

"It might be necessary."

"I don't know that she'd be able to add anything to what I might say."

"You never know. It's worth checking. Anyway," said Mahmoud, who didn't like any detail to escape him, "the investigation ought to be done properly."

"Yes, it ought. Both sides will be watching it."

"Both sides?"

"Copts and Moslems."

Owen told Mahmoud about the things that had been occupying him recently.

"The best thing you could do would be to find he died of a heart attack."

"There'll have to be an autopsy. Keep your fingers crossed."

They watched a camel coming down the street towards them. It was heavily loaded with berseem, green forage for the cab horses in the squares. The load extended so far across the camel that it brushed the walls on both sides of the narrow street. Advancing towards it was a tiny donkey almost buried under a load of firewood. The load was as big as a small haystack. On top of it sat the donkey's owner, an old Arab dressed in a dirty white galabeah. The two animals met. Neither would, neither could, give way, the camel because it was stuck between the walls, the donkey because it was so crushed under its huge load that it was quite incapable of manoeuvring. Both drivers swore at each other and interested spectators came out of the houses to watch. Eventually the drivers were persuaded to try to edge the animals past each other. In doing so the donkey lost some of its firewood and the camel some of its berseem. The wood fell among the pots of a small shopkeeper who came out of his shop in a fury and belaboured both animals. They stuck. Neither could move forwards or backwards despite the best help of observers. The rest of the inhabitants of the street came out to help, including the people smoking water-pipes in the dark inner rooms of the café. Mahmoud shifted his chair so that he could see better.

"This could take a long time," he said.

The indignant cries of the drivers rose to the heavens where they mingled with the shouts of the onlookers, who for some reason all felt compelled to offer their advice at the top of their voices. The din was terrific. Owen looked on the scene almost with affection. He loved the daily dramas of the Cairo streets in which high positions were taken as in a Greek tragedy but in which no one was ever really hurt. Would that all Egyptian conflicts were like that, he said to himself. He was thinking of the matter of the dog, but was beginning, now, to have a slightly uneasy feeling about the Zikr.

"It would be good if both these cases were out of the way before the twenty-fifth."

"Why?"

"It's the Coptic Easter. And the Moulid of the Sheikh el-Herera."

"And the Sham el-Nessim," said Mahmoud, "you've forgotten that."

The spring festival.

"Christ. Is that on too?"

"This year, yes."

"Bloody hell!"

"I'll try and sort it out before then," said Mahmoud, still watching the drama. "You'll have sorted out the dog business by then, too."

"Yes, but it mightn't help."

Along the street one of the onlookers was taking off his trousers. This usually meant business in Egypt. Trousers, especially good ones, were prestigious possessions and no one would want to risk spoiling them by involving them in action. The onlooker, now trouserless, took hold of the donkey firmly by the head, turned it round, despite the protests of its owner, and began to lead it back up the street. It passed the café and turned up a side street. The camel resumed its passage, not, however, without incident. As it approached the café it suddenly became apparent that its load would sweep all before it. Patrons, including Owen and Mahmoud, hurriedly rushed chairs and tables inside. The camel went past. At the junction with the side street it stopped and the driver looked back. Clearly he was thinking about the spilt berseem. Vigorous cries dissuaded him from going back. After a few moments' hesitation he shrugged his shoulders and went on. Meanwhile, the donkey was led back up the street and restored to its owner. By the time it reached the scene of the blockage both the spilt berseem and the spilt firewood had gone.

"Right!" said Mahmoud. "I'll do my best. I'll start at once with the principal witness."

"Who's that?" asked Owen.

"You," said Mahmoud.

"You don't remember anything?"

"More than what I've told you? Sorry."

"We've got the general picture," said Mahmoud. "It's the particulars I'm after."

"I know," said Owen humbly.

"You saw this Zikr afterwards. The dead one, I mean. So you know what he looked like. Do you remember seeing him before? When he was dancing?"

"Sort of," said Owen vaguely.

"He had knives and spears sticking out all over him."

"Lots of them did!" protested Owen.

"This one especially. Look, I'll help you. He had a spear sticking into his front chest. A three-foot handle. At least three feet. It must have been waggling about."

"Can't remember."

"I would have thought it would have got in the way, dancing."

Owen shut his eyes.

"I can't picture it," he said.

"It doesn't jog your memory?"

"No." Owen shook his head. "I'm sorry," he said.

Mahmoud sighed.

"There was so much happening." Owen protested. "I've told you."

"Yes, you've given me the general picture very well. Let's try again. When did you first become conscious of the Zikr?"

"When he didn't get up. After a long time."

"Where was he? When he was lying down, I mean."

"About four or five yards in front of me to my left. There, as it were."

Owen pointed to where a flea-ridden dog was scratching itself in the dust. A dog. He winced.

"Good!" said Mahmoud encouragingly. "About four or five yards to your left."

"He was lying in a heap."

"Fine. And if he was lying there he might well have been dancing there. You said they sank down more or less where they were."

"That's how it seemed to me. At the time."

"Try to call up the scene," said Mahmoud patiently, "with them all dancing. Got it? Right. Well now, look in your mind a little to your left. Four yards, five yards? Six yards?"

"I'm trying. I just don't see it very clearly. I thought I did."

"Over to your left. A big dervish with a spear sticking out of his chest."

After a moment or two Owen said: "I think I've got him."

"What is he doing?"

"Dancing."

"How is he dancing?"

"Jumping up and down. I think."

"Is he turning round? Whirling?"

"A bit."

"Does the spear hit anyone? Get in the way?"

"It's not really there," said Owen. "I don't really see it. I can sort of imagine it when you speak."

"But you're not really remembering it?"

"No."

Mahmoud sighed.

"As a Mamur Zapt you may be all right," he said. "As a witness you're useless."

"I know."

Owen felt humbled. A murder, possibly, had happened four or five yards away under his very eyes and he couldn't remember a thing. He hadn't even noticed it. Perhaps, he told himself determinedly, there had been nothing to notice.

"We don't know anything happened," he said to Mahmoud.

"Yes, but we know he was there," said Mahmoud, "and even that could be in doubt if we went by your evidence."

"It's not very good, is it?" said Owen. "A police officer and not remember a thing."

Mahmoud laughed.

"I don't know that I'd have done any better. It just goes to show."

"What are you going to do now?"

"Try the next witness. See if she remembers any better."

"She?"

"Miss—" Mahmoud stumbled a little. What he was trying to say was Postlethwaite.

"Surely you don't need to see her?"

"I'm afraid I do."

"There must be other witnesses."

"And I shall get to them. But it was fresh to her eyes and she"—said Mahmoud pointedly—"may remember more."

Owen was silent. He hadn't realized it would come to this. He considered how Miss Postlethwaite would feel about being involved in a police inquiry. Or, more to the point, how her uncle would feel about it. Or, even more to the point, how the Consul-General would react.

"Are you sure?" he said. "I mean, she's hardly likely to be able to add anything to what I—"

"You want to bet?" asked Mahmoud.

"Yes," said Jane Postlethwaite. "I remember the man very well. I'd noticed him earlier because he was so—involved. He put everything into his dancing. He was a big man, rather darker than most of the Zikr—that would be, I expect"—looking at Owen for confirmation—"because he came from the south, although he wasn't really a Nubian, he wasn't as dark as that, a mixture, I suppose. Anyway, he threw himself into his dancing rather like a great big child. He seemed a bit like an overgrown boy, he had that sort of childlike face. I'd noticed him because he was bounding away so enthusiastically. And then when he started sticking knives into himself I could hardly believe my eyes. And that spear!"

Jane Postlethwaite shuddered a little at the recollection but it was not so much in sympathetic trepidation as in identification. She saw it all so vividly.

Mahmoud looked at Owen triumphantly.

"Yes, that spear," he said. "How did he manage with it, Miss Postlethwaite? I would have thought it would have knocked into people as he was dancing."

"It did once or twice. I thought it would hurt him but it didn't seem to. And then, you see, it wasn't sticking out horizontally. He'd thrust it into himself from above. He held it up—I saw him, it was so that everyone could see—up in front of him, like this"—Miss Postlethwaite demonstrated—"and then he pulled it down into his chest. The handle was sticking upwards, if anything. And then he was so big, it was over most people's heads."

This time Owen took care not to meet Mahmoud's eyes. Miss Postlethwaite seemed to recall with amazing facility. She had agreed without hesitation when he had asked her, diffidently, whether she would be willing to make herself available for questioning. "Of course!" she had replied. "It's my duty." "It won't be me who's asking the questions," he had said, "it will be a friend of mine, Mr. el-Zaki, from the Parquet." He had explained how the legal system differed from that in Britain. "In any case," Jane Postlethwaite had said, "it wouldn't have been proper for you to question me, would it? I mean, you were involved yourself. I expect you're a witness too. Are you, Captain Owen? Oh, perhaps you'd better not tell me anything about it. Otherwise you might influence what I say and that wouldn't be right, would it?"

To give things as light a touch as possible, Mahmoud had interviewed her in her hotel, and he had asked Owen to be with him. Owen knew very well why he wanted this. It wasn't that he doubted his own ability or needed reinforcement. Rather, it was a simple precautionary measure, advisable when an Egyptian was questioning one of the British community, especially a visitor of some importance. Owen had agreed, though with a certain apprehension. They would be sure to meet John Postlethwaite, he thought, and the MP would be sure to take up the issue with him. When they arrived at the hotel his worst fears appeared to have been realized, for there, waiting for them in the vestibule, was Postlethwaite himself.

"Young man!" he said formidably, and Owen feared the worst.

"I must apologize, sir," he said hastily. "It was quite wrong of me to expose Miss Postlethwaite to the possibility of such a distressing incident."

"Ay," said the MP, "it was."

He produced the look which had crushed ministers. Owen recognized it at once and appeared suitably daunted. Unexpectedly, Mr. Postlethwaite seemed mollified.

"Well, you're not trying to wriggle out of it at any rate," he said.

"My fault entirely, sir."

Mr. Postlethwaite sighed.

"Look, lad," he said, "you're young and you don't know any better. But you don't say things like that. Not if you want to get on in government service. It's always somebody else's fault. Got it? I'll take this up with you some other time. You need a bit of advice."

He spotted Mahmoud.

"This is Mr. el-Zaki, I take it? How do you do, Mr. el-Zaki." They shook hands. "I don't altogether follow this Parquet business, but it sounds a bit like the Scottish system to me."

"You're quite right," said Owen, pleased. "It is."

"It's not a bad system," said Mr. Postlethwaite. "At least you know who's responsible for what."

Jane Postlethwaite appeared in the doorway.

"I hope you've not been pitching into Captain Owen, Uncle," she said.

"A bit," said John Postlethwaite, exaggerating. Owen suspected that he liked to play the role of the hard man with his niece; and that she was not deceived in the least.

"I've pitched into the departments," he said with relish. He winked at Owen. "Now they'll know what to expect if they try to pull the wool over my eyes."

"Get them on the run," advised Jane Postlethwaite. "That's half the battle."

Owen was a little surprised at this display of administrative savoir-faire but then realized that she was probably repeating one of her uncle's maxims. Mr. Postlethwaite endorsed it anyway.

"That's right," he said.

His niece laid a hand on his arm.

"Now, Uncle," she said, "you'd better get back to your memos. Once you've got them on the run, keep them on the run."

"And that's true too," said John Postlethwaite, going happily off up the stairs.

Jane Postlethwaite led them into a small room which the hotel manager had made available. The shutters had been closed, which kept the room fairly cool; but the air was lukewarm and inert and the fans useless, so after a while she pushed the shutters right open and they sat by the window.

"It is fortunate for us that you were watching, Miss Postlethwaite," said Mahmoud, "and that you're such a good observer."

"Thank you. I wasn't really watching him particularly, you know. It was just that I couldn't help noticing him. He was so striking. So big, and so—rapt."

"Did you notice him towards the end of the dance? Just before he collapsed?"

"Yes. He was bounding about and I kept thinking: Surely he can't keep this up, not with all those knives and things sticking in him. But he did. He kept jumping away. Then he seemed to falter. There was a man near him and I thought he had bumped into him, because he, the Zikr, I mean, seemed to stumble. And then all his strength seemed to go out of him and he just slumped down. I think his fatigue had just caught up with him. Other Zikr were collapsing too, at that point."

"The man who was standing near him, the one he bumped into or might have bumped into, was he another Zikr?"

"Oh no. He was one of—the audience, I suppose I should say, one of the onlookers, anyway. He had sort of strayed into the ring, been drawn in, I suppose, like so many others. There were lots of them, you know, ordinary people. They pressed forward during the dancing and then they began to join in. It was very infectious. I felt quite like joining in myself. Only I thought Captain Owen would not approve of me."

She gave Owen a look which he considered afterwards he could only describe as arch.

Mahmoud, however, was concentrating.

"This particular onlooker, the one the Zikr nearly bumped into, was he joining in?"

"No. He was just standing there. That is why I noticed him. I thought he was, well, you know, a bit dazed or something, bowled over by it all. I was afraid he would get in the way. And then, when the Zikr stumbled, I thought he had got in the way."

"Could you describe him for us, Miss Postlethwaite?" Mahmoud asked. "What was he wearing, for instance?"

"Oh, ordinary clothes."

"Ordinary Western clothes or ordinary Egyptian clothes?"

"How silly I am. Of course. Ordinary Egyptian clothes. A long gown. A—galabeah, is it?"

"You're picking up our language well, Miss Postlethwaite," said Mahmoud encouragingly. "Galabeah is quite right. A blue one?"

"No. Darker than that. Grey? Black?"

"Are you sure about that, Miss Postlethwaite?" Owen interposed.

"Well, not absolutely. It was dark by then and hard to see in the light. It was just that in comparison with the others his seemed dark."

"Did you see what kind of turban he was wearing?"

"I am afraid not. I'm sorry. One turban is much like another to me. Darkish, anyway. Like his gown."

Owen exchanged surreptitious glances with Mahmoud. It was early yet but he was already beginning to have a sinking feeling.

"Anything else, Miss Postlethwaite?" asked Mahmoud.

"Not really. I saw him only fleetingly."

"How old was he?"

"Thirty, forty—"

"You saw his face?"

"I must have," said Jane, concentrating. After a moment or two she shook her head. "I don't remember it at all clearly, I'm afraid."

"Hands?"

"Hands?" said Jane, startled.

"Sometimes they are distinctive."

"Yes," said Jane, looking at him with interest. "Yes, they are. Well, I did see his hands, but there was nothing distinctive about them. It was just—"

She broke off and thought for a moment. "I don't remember *his* hands," she said at last, "but I do remember hers."

"Hers?"

"The woman's."

"What woman's?"

"Don't you know?" said Jane, surprised. "Oh, I see, you're testing me. The woman he was with."

Mahmoud recovered first.

"Tell us about this woman, please, Miss Postlethwaite," he asked.

"Right," said Jane obediently. "Well, we were in a sort of enclosure, you know, masked off by ropes. During the dancing this woman came right up beside me, outside the enclosure—I was at the very end of the row, next to the rope, there was a carpet hung over it, too, which made it into a sort of wall—and put her hand on the rope just in front of me. That's why I saw it in the first place. But then, of course, I noticed it. She had such lovely hand-painting. Lots of Egyptian women do, don't they?"

"Yes," said Mahmoud, "although it's going out now, or so my mother says."

"Does she herself hand-paint?" asked Jane.

"No!" said Mahmoud, immensely amused at the thought of his rather Westernized mother engaging in the traditional Egyptian arts. "It's not confined to the poorer classes but it's certainly most common there. You find it generally where the old customs are strongest."

"Such beautiful patterns!" said Jane enthusiastically.

"In general?" asked Mahmoud. "Or just in the case of the woman you saw beside the enclosure?"

"Both!" said Jane. "But I noticed the woman because I thought her patterns were especially lovely. She didn't paint the whole palm, you know, not like they usually do, she just sort of sketched it in and then echoed it around the knuckles and nails. But what really caught my eye were her wrists. She had a most intricate pattern around them, all in delicate blue, not the usual blue of the poorer women, and not that rich orangey-red you often see. It ran round her wrist in a series of hooks and crosses all linked together, like a sort of painted bracelet."

"Crosses?" said Owen. He was quite sure about the sinking feeling now.

"Yes. Small square ones. That's a traditional pattern too, isn't it?"

"Yes," said Owen, "especially among some people."

Mahmoud was pleased.

"You are a most excellent observer, Miss Postlethwaite," he told her warmly.

"I could hardly help noticing, could I?" said Jane, half-apologetically. "It was right before my eyes."

"Yes, but not everyone notices what's right in front of their eyes."

Owen kept his own eyes looking firmly out of the window.

"Can you tell us anything else about this woman, Miss Postlethwaite?" asked Mahmoud.

"Not really," said Jane. "She was dressed from head to foot in one of those black gowns. I suppose I wouldn't even have seen her hand if she had not put it on the rope. The only thing—" She hesitated.

"Yes?" prompted Mahmoud.

"The only thing I remember," she said, "was the smell."

"What sort of smell?"

"Scent."

"She had a lot of perfume on?"

"No. Not exactly. Not in that way."

"Distinctive? A distinctive perfume? Heavy, perhaps?"

Jane shook her head.

"Not really. I don't quite know what it was. Perhaps it was where it was that surprised me."

"Where it was?"

"Yes. It wasn't on her wrist or on her throat, not where you'd usually put it. In fact, it wasn't on her at all. It was on her sleeve. And—not just on one part. All over her sleeve."

"Ah."

"That means something to you, does it?" she said, looking at Mahmoud.

"It might. Tell me—can you remember—was it one perfume or different ones?"

"How clever of you. Different ones. She had been trying them on, you think? But on her sleeve?"

"You've been very helpful, Miss Postlethwaite," said Mahmoud. "Truly very helpful."

"Is it important?" asked Jane. "I don't quite see—"

"It might be," said Mahmoud. "Now, can we just go back a

little. At a certain point you became aware of this lady placing her hand on the rope. When exactly was that?"

"I can't say exactly. Towards the end of the dancing? Yes, it must have been towards the end because at the start, you know, the women were at the back, it was the men who were at the front, and then as the dancing went on everyone became sort of drawn in and some of the women came forward, though of course they didn't actually join in the dancing or anything like that, except to cry out and encourage the dancers."

"And that was when this woman came forward?"

"Yes."

"With the man?"

"Oh no. He was already there. So far forward that he was almost part of the dance."

"When did they meet up, then?" asked Mahmoud. "You spoke of her as being with him."

"Afterwards. They left together."

"When the Zikr collapsed?"

"Yes. He stepped back into the crowd. I think he realized that it was partly his fault, that he had bumped into the Zikr. I mean, he shouldn't really have been there, should he? He was just getting in the way. He stepped back right in front of me, I couldn't see the dancers for a moment or two, that's how I remember, but then the crowd let him in and he slipped back along the rope."

"Where the woman was waiting?"

"Yes. It seemed like that, because as soon as he got to her she turned and left with him. I was aware of it because she had been partly blocking my vision and when she left I could see the little boys bringing fire."

Deep in the recess of the hotel a gong sounded and Miss Postlethwaite stirred slightly. A splendid suffragi in a red sash appeared at the door. Mahmoud rose to his feet and put out his hand.

"Thank you very much, Miss Postlethwaite," he said. "You have been an immense help."

"I have? Oh, I am so pleased."

"You are an excellent observer."

"I just notice what I see."

"Not everyone does."

Mahmoud could not forbear a glance in Owen's direction.

"Oh, of course," said Jane Postlethwaite, catching the glance and misinterpreting it. "You will already know all this. Captain Owen will have told you."

"Not quite all, Miss Postlethwaite," said Mahmoud, "not quite all."

CHAPTER 4

It was safe to assume in Cairo that nothing you did would go unobserved. No matter how private the occasion or how secret the place, someone would be bound to be watching. So it was with the matter of the dog. It was not long before Georgiades, Owen's agent, had found not one but two witnesses. Not only that; the accounts of the witnesses—and this was definitely unusual in Cairo—roughly corresponded.

The first was an old man, an Arab, who lived in the cemetery. Georgiades showed Owen where he lived. It was in a space between two gravestones beneath the rubble of a collapsed tomb. Peering down between the stones Owen saw a hole about five feet deep and four feet square. It was in there that the old man lived. Apart from a worn rush mat he had no provisions, but the hole at least kept him cool during the hot weather and sheltered him from the wind during the khamsin. He had a short, torn galabeah and thin, bird-like legs. His face was scruffy with grey stubble and his eyes, as they looked up towards the light, were so red with disease that the first question was whether he could have seen what he claimed he had.

During the night, he said, men had come.

Men? Yes, he was adamant. Four or five of them, carrying something. They had stopped some way from the tomb. He could show them. No, he had not gone himself to the place, he had been frightened, thinking that perhaps they were carrying a corpse. The Copts would have been angry with him if they had seen him. They would think he had been observing their secret rites. So he had kept well away from them, hidden among the rubble, but he had definitely seen them, a small group of men in the light of the moon.

Had they gone to the tomb? Did he know which tomb? Yes, he did. It was the tomb of Andrus. He knew Andrus because the Copt had often chided him when he saw him among the tombs; but he had sometimes given him alms, too. He knew the tomb because he had sometimes seen Andrus there, praying. It was a holy place and he, the old man, often liked to sit there, especially when the sun had just moved off the wall, because then he could sit there with his back against the wall and the stone would warm his back. He knew the tomb and he had seen the men going there.

Did they go in? Yes, but not for long. It was a holy place and perhaps they had been frightened. He had heard the door squeak and then they had all come running down the stairs and made off into the rubble.

He had seen the men in the moonlight: what sort of men were they? Bad men. Only bad men would do a thing like that. To come at night to the Place of the Dead! And there to do mischief. Bad men. Bad men.

But what sort of men were they? Were they—and this was the tricky question—were they Copts? Or Moslems? The old man was silent. Owen tried again. How were they dressed? In galabeahs or in trousers? Alas, the old man could not see. He had been far away and it had been dark. Yet he had seen the men in the light of the moon. The old man became confused and fell silent.

Owen tried a different tack. Did they come as men who knew the necropolis, or did they hesitate, wondering which way to go? The old man thought they knew. But then he thought that they had stopped before going to the tomb because perhaps they had not been quite sure which one it was.

His attention began to wander and it soon became apparent that there was no point in questioning him further.

The second witness was a small boy. There were lots of small boys in the necropolis. Not all of them were abandoned orphans. Some of them had loose connections with families in the poor districts which surrounded the cemetery. The families were often unable to sustain too many children and the older ones sometimes drifted away into a kind of semi-independence.

The girls became household servants or prostitutes. The boys made for the wilderness of the necropolis. Like the old man, they sustained themselves by begging from the wealthy Copts and fighting for scraps of food among the garbage tossed out into the cemetery from the more well-to-do Moslem houses along its western side. They moved in gangs, like the packs of dogs of which there were plenty in the necropolis, and with which they had a curious relationship, half-inimical, half-tolerated, sharing a mutual signalling system which alerted them at once to any intruders.

Aware of newcomers though they might be, that did not make them more ready to come forward. Even though they had already made Georgiades's acquaintance, when he appeared with Owen they remained hidden among the stones, and he had to have recourse to the strategy which had worked before. He settled himself comfortably on the edge of a tomb and began to toss a coin casually into the air.

He went on tossing for about ten minutes, and only then did the first heads begin to appear. Slowly they moved forward until there was a ring of little boys surrounding them, all keeping at safe fleeing distance. At last Georgiades's contact came out of hiding. Once he had made his move he came boldly forward, but stopped just beyond arm's length.

"Who is this man?" he said, pointing at Owen.

"He's a friend of mine," said Georgiades.

"I know him," said the boy. "He's the Mamur Zapt."

"Like I said. He's a friend of mine."

"You have powerful friends."

"I need them."

The boy looked doubtful.

"It is dangerous to have powerful friends," he said.

"Worse to have powerful enemies."

"He couldn't touch me."

"I wouldn't want to touch you," said Owen.

The boy seemed more than half-inclined to retreat back among the stones. Georgiades began to toss his coin speculatively.

"Does he pay you?" said the boy suddenly.

"Not enough," said Georgiades.

That seemed to reassure the child.

"One never gets enough," he said, with the air of an old man.

"One has to live by one's wits."

"Will he pay me, too?"

"I will pay you," said Owen, "if you tell me what I want to know."

The boy still did not come forward.

"I am afraid," he said.

"I shall not hurt you," said Owen.

"It's not you I'm afraid of."

"Who are you afraid of?"

"The big man with his knife. Also the holy one."

"Which one are you afraid of most?" asked Georgiades.

The boy considered.

"The holy one," he said at last. "The other, though big, is slow. He would never catch me. The holy one has many men. He might get one I did not know to seize me and hold me so that he could beat me. Also," he added as an afterthought, "the holy one might call down great curses on me."

"If you tell me the truth," said Owen, "I will give you something which will heal both the beatings and the curses."

"How much?" said the boy practically.

Owen mentioned a sum.

The boy turned away disappointed.

"It is not worth us talking."

"It is always worth talking," said Georgiades, flipping his coin in the air.

"Not for that it isn't."

"No?"

Georgiades continued to flip.

After a little while the boy said: "For two such coins I might be willing."

Georgiades was so shocked by the suggestion that he missed his catch, almost, and had to fumble to stop the coin from falling on the ground, where it might have rolled away to join the lost treasures of the pharaohs; but fortunately he recovered.

"Three piastres I might manage," said Georgiades grudgingly, "if the information is good. The fourth piastre—well, who knows, you might be able to tell me something later on."

The boy accepted three piastres; one paid in advance, one

paid when he came close enough for Georgiades to catch hold of him, and one to be paid after he had given his information. The fourth piastre was to be a bonus depending on the extent and quality of the information.

The story in outline was the same. The men had come into the necropolis late at night and had made their way towards the house of Andrus joking uneasily and talking loudly among themselves. They had quietened down as they approached the tomb and the last part of the journey had been covered in silence. They had stopped when they were some way short of their objective. The boy said it was because several of the men were afraid there might be spirits lingering about the tomb who might be hostile towards them because they weren't Christian. They had succeeded in infecting the others with their fear and in the end no one had wanted to go on. Then one of them had said that it would be a shame to go back again without having done anything now that they had come so far, and that he was not afraid, especially as the spirits would be bound to be weak ones, being Coptic. He would go by himself if no one would go with him. No one would go with him and the man became angry, saying they were cowards and weaklings and feeble of faith. Still no one would go with him and in the end he had taken the bundle himself. He had gone to the tomb alone.

Alone? Yes, said the boy, alone. Not with the others? No, not with the others. They had watched from afar.

Owen was inclined to believe him. His account was more circumstantial than the old man's. He reported conversation, too, which suggested that he or his informants had gone closer to the men. It might all be invention, the sort of stuff that he thought the Mamur Zapt would like to hear, but on the whole the account rang true.

What happened then? While the man was delivering the bundle a door had scraped along the stone making a loud, grating sound. The man had come rushing down the steps in a fright and all the men had run off into the darkness. They had scattered and some of them had lost their way and had not been able to get out of the necropolis till morning. The boy reported this with a trace of contempt in his voice, as of a professional speaking about amateurs.

Owen asked the boy if he had seen the nature of the bundle.

The boy said no, but left little doubt that then or later he had learned what it contained. Had he seen the men? Again the boy said no. He hesitated slightly, however, and Owen got the impression he was holding something back. He pressed him but got no response.

The boy tugged at Georgiades's arm.

"Can I have my money?" he said.

Georgiades fumbled in his pocket and produced the third piastre.

"What you have told us is certainly worth three piastres," he said. "The question is, is it worth four?"

He looked at Owen.

"In itself it isn't," said Owen, "but if we give it him perhaps he will remember us and come to us again."

Georgiades found a fourth piastre and gave it to the boy.

"This is how I became poor," he said.

The boy, released, moved a little further off, out of reach, but did not go away. He was looking at Owen.

"I have heard of you," he said.

"What have you heard?"

The boy did not reply directly.

"My mother's brother works for you," he said suddenly.

"His name?"

"Yussuf."

Yussuf was one of the office bearers.

"I know him well," said Owen.

"Too well," added Georgiades.

"How is your mother?" asked Owen politely.

"She is angry with Yussuf."

"Why?"

"He has put away his wife. Now he has no woman and he expects her to clean for him."

"I will speak to Yussuf."

"For God's sake, don't add to his problems," Georgiades counselled, "or the coffee will get even worse."

"Do not tell him I spoke with you," said the boy.

Owen promised he wouldn't.

"It shall be a secret between us," he said, "as with all else you have told me. And anything further you tell me," he added, watching the boy.

"I am afraid," the boy said.

"The holy one?"

The boy did not reply.

"Are you afraid he might punish you if he hears you have spoken with me?"

The boy glanced over his shoulder at the other boys behind him in the stones.

"They need not hear. They need not know."

"They will tell him that I have spoken with you."

"He will ask, and you will tell him all that you have told us."

"That is right," said the boy.

"And he will not mind because so far you have not told us anything that touches him."

The boy was silent.

"He need not know," said Owen, "if you tell us a little more."

The boy was torn.

"I would tell you—"

"Tell us," said Owen. "It is a dangerous thing to have powerful friends. But sometimes it is a good thing."

"They were his men."

"The holy one's? The men who came to the Place of the Dead?"

The boy nodded.

"Who is this holy one?" asked Georgiades.

The boy did not reply at once. He seemed to be studying the marks his toe traced in the sand. Owen thought at first that they might be intended as a message, but of course the boy could not write.

Then he lifted his head and looked Owen straight in the eye.

"The Sheikh Osman Rahman."

"Did he send them?"

The boy pulled away.

"I can say no more. I must go. They will suspect."

"Very well. You have helped me," said Owen, "and I shall not forget."

The boy stepped back towards them.

"Offer me money," he said to Georgiades.

Georgiades took out another piastre.

"That is not enough. Two."

Georgiades obliged.

"Not like that," said the boy impatiently. "As you did."

Georgiades cottoned on. He took the large double piastre coin between forefinger and thumb and showed it to the boy in exaggerated fashion. The boy looked at it as if mesmerized and allowed himself to be drawn slowly forward. Then, as Georgiades reached out a hand for him, he kicked Georgiades smartly on the shin, knocked the coin out of his hand, scooped it up in a flash out of the sand and sprang away laughing.

For a moment he stood there trilling triumphantly. Then he disappeared into the stones with his fellows.

Georgiades rubbed his shin and cursed. Even though the kick had been delivered with the bare foot it had still hurt.

"Little sod," he said. "Smart little sod," he added admiringly.

"Who is this woman, anyway?" demanded Zeinab.

"I told you. She's the niece of this MP who's visiting us."

"What is she doing here?"

"Keeping him company, I suppose. Having a holiday."

"She's come here to get a husband. Like all the others."

"I wouldn't have thought so. She's not like them."

This was a mistake.

"How is she not like them?" Zeinab asked.

Owen floundered.

"Well, she's quieter. More retiring."

"She doesn't seem to have retired so far," said Zeinab. "What's she like? Is she beautiful?"

"No. She's not beautiful. I don't know what she's like, really. Mostly she's been under that hat."

"Cunning."

Owen looked at the memo incredulously. It came from Accounts, and it said:

To the Mamur Zapt:

Camel Watering

We notice there have been two recent transfers of sums from the Camel Watering Account to the Curbash Compensation Fund. We assume these transfers to have been made in error. We remind the Mamur Zapt that he has no capacity to vire.

"What the hell does that mean?"

"It means that you can't switch money from other accounts into the Curbash Compensation Fund," said Nikos.

"Why not?"

"Because you have no capacity to vire."

"What the hell's that?"

"It means to take money which is under one heading and put it under another. It's an accounting term."

"I can't switch money from one account to another because I can't switch money from one account to another. Is that it?"

"Exactly."

"But I've always done it."

"And now they've found out."

"But I need to. The accounts are all wrong otherwise."

"If I were you," said Nikos, "I wouldn't tell them that."

"Who the hell do they think they are? I can vire if I want to."

"No," said Nikos, "you can't. The restriction on viring was one of Cromer's first measures. It's a basic accounting principle. Ask Postlethwaite."

"Well, I don't know that I'll take it up with him—"

"If I were you I wouldn't take it up. It's one of the things they're very hot on."

"Yes, but we need the money."

"You'd better talk to Garvin. Though I don't know that that will do much good."

"About that hedgehog of yours," said Cairns-Grant, the forensic pathologist.

"What?" said Owen, startled.

Cairns-Grant chuckled, pleased at the success of his little joke.

"That Zikr. The one with all the spikes in him."

He wiped his mouth with his napkin and signalled to Owen to take the seat opposite him. He was still at the soup stage and was, indeed, having full Sudani, which was the main reason why Owen went to the Sporting Club for lunch.

"You've done the autopsy?"

"Yes. Very straightforward."

There was a touch of regret, even reproach, in Cairns-Grant's voice.

"Sorry."

"Never mind," said Cairns-Grant comfortingly. "You're doing very well. It's not every day you get a Zikr with knives all over. It's out of the common run. I've great hopes of you."

The waiter, who knew Owen's preferences, brought him the full Sudani.

"What did you find?"

"First, that it wasn't one of the blades still sticking in him that killed him. None of them went near a vital place. The Zikr may get carried away," said Cairns-Grant, "but they're not daft."

"They know where to put the blade in?"

"Ay."

"Even so—"

"I know what you're thinking. Loss of blood. Well, there's less of that than you might think. I remember when I first came out here being able to check some Zikr over after they had finished their dance. The Government wanted evidence that it was excessive and dangerous. Well, I knew some of the sheikhs so I got them to let me give their men a checkover. There was very little bleeding and when the blades were retracted the wounds healed very quickly. It took a week or two, of course, but even immediately after the dancing most of them were able to walk around quite normally. I dare say you noticed that yourself?"

"Yes," said Owen, remembering.

"They're strong," Cairns-Grant acknowledged, finishing his soup and putting down his spoon. "They're big strong laddies and very fit. But there must be another factor. And I don't know what it is."

He looked thoughtfully into space. The waiters, on whom he had the same effect as he did on Owen, thought the gaze was meant for them and rushed to bring him his chops.

"Ay, well," he said, recovering and glancing down at his chops, "that's another story."

"How was he killed, then?"

"We found another stab wound. It penetrated the heart."

"Not one of the blades still sticking in?" said Owen.

"No."

"Fallen out?"

Cairns-Grant shook his head.

"Unlikely. Very deep. Inserted with considerable force. It would have taken force to pull it out."

"Removed, then?"

"Yes."

"Someone else, then. Not self-inflicted."

"No doubt about it," said Cairns-Grant. "Inserted from behind."

Owen nodded.

"Okay," he said. "Thanks."

"An upward thrust," said Cairns-Grant, "delivered by somebody small. About five feet six or five feet eight. I've tried it out."

"He would have died at once, presumably?"

"Yes."

"It must have been someone in the dance, then."

"Another Zikr?"

"Someone who joined the dance," said Owen.

"Got someone who fits?"

"Yes."

"Good," said Cairns-Grant. "Good." He examined his chops with a view to dissection. "Well, young man," he said, reaching out for his knife and fork, "you would seem to have a murder on your hands. Yes, definitely."

CHAPTER 5

They met at the Bab es Zuweyla, one of the old gates of Cairo, now the centre of the native city. As they approached the gate the street narrowed and became more mediaeval. The houses with their heavy wooden windows leaned over the street until they almost touched in the middle, making it always cool and dark. At ground level the street was lined with traditional little native shops, most of them carpenters, it seemed; and as they came through the Tentmakers' Bazaar, with its gay awnings and saddle-cloth and leather work, they saw ahead of them in the archway of the gate the gleam of the blue tiles of the tiny dervish mosque.

Most of the bazaars were on the other side of the gate. There were nine main ones: the Silk Bazaar, the Cotton Bazaar, the Tunisian and Algerian Bazaar, the Silversmiths' and Goldsmiths' Bazaar, the Sudanese Bazaar, the Brass Bazaar, the Shoemakers' Bazaar, the Turkish Bazaar, and the Scentmakers' Bazaar.

The Scentmakers' Bazaar, which was where Mahmoud was taking them, was one of the oldest and most traditional of the bazaars. The shops were mere cupboards, little dark recesses, six feet high, six deep and four wide, lined with shelves, in front of which was a long, low counter on which the owner sat, like some carved idol in a niche.

Beside him on the counter were large dirty bottles of gilt glass from which he would take out the stoppers and daub them on the sleeves of passers-by. On his other side was an array of cheap, gaudy small bottles for the scent he sold; and on the floor in front of him were ivory balls with cavities for scent.

Behind him, on the shelves of his dark recess, were large brown bottles criss-crossed with gold and rows of foolish otto-of-roses bottles, cut and gilt, but with hardly more inside than a thermometer. Sometimes, too, there was an assistant, a boy for fetching the bottles, a woman for modelling the perfume, but always, in this most traditional of bazaars, totally concealed in shapeless black.

Mahmoud, hesitantly, had asked Owen if Zeinab could possibly come too. Owen had put it to her and, slightly to his surprise, she had agreed. The Scentmakers' Bazaar was not normally a place she would have allowed herself to have been seen dead in. Like many well-to-do Cairenes, she took her perfumes, with her fashions, direct from Paris. However, on this occasion she was intrigued and agreed readily enough.

As soon as they began to walk along the shops Owen was very glad that she had come. She addressed herself to the task with her usual imperiousness and dragged Owen and Mahmoud along in her wake. She entered into technical discussions with the shopkeepers in a way totally beyond the capacity of Owen and Mahmoud, explaining that while she normally wore only French perfume, she was considering experimenting with a combination of French and Arab scents: *"une vraie cairéenne, n'est-ce pas?"* She treated coldly all attempts to dab the scent on her own sleeve, rejected any suggestion that it could suitably be tried out on Owen and Mahmoud, and insisted that it be tested on a woman, an assistant, perhaps, or, preferably, the shopkeeper's wife, a suggestion which, with its hint of superiority, would have had shopkeepers in the more Westernized parts of the city grovelling but was treated simply commercially in the bazaar.

There were three Coptic scentmakers in the bazaar. One was an elderly, rather exhausted man who was unable to produce either assistant or wife and had to borrow a lady from his neighbour for the purpose. One was a middle-aged man, rather corpulent, who sent a message into the depths behind his recess which finally produced an abashed female servant; and one was a spare man in young middle age who had his wife helping him in the shop. She was used to helping with such requests and come forward at once when asked.

Zeinab spent a lot of time with this shopkeeper. Several of his perfumes seemed promising and in the end she took away samples in three small bottles and promised that she would return when she had tried them out. She asked the shopkeeper's name so that she would know to whom to send her servant. It was Zoser.

Zoser served her politely but with an air of detachment, as if his mind was on higher things. There was an ascetic quality about him. He gave the impression that he had come straight from fasting; and there was a mild hint of irritation at his fast being interrupted.

At the last moment Zeinab dithered. She wanted to try just once again a perfume she had already rejected. When Zoser dabbed a little on his wife's sleeve she took the sleeve and held it up to her nose. The wife obligingly lifted her arm and for the first time there was a flash of something pale, as if to show that there really was flesh and blood beneath the shapeless black garment.

"No," said Zeinab, "no, I think I was right after all. I'll just take these."

They continued on along the line of booths, each with its owner sitting on the counter among his stained, dirty jars like some vast black spider, past the long, carpet-covered benches in front of them with the rows of men drinking coffee and smoking and talking, past the assorted smells of rose and jasmin, amber and banana, past the odd little restaurants with their grand brass jugs of hot water, their servants hurrying with coffee in glasses to some merchant about to strike a deal, past all this and then suddenly through the arch of the Bab es Zuweyla with its two soaring and fantastic minarets and out once more into the Tentmakers' Bazaar with its donkey-saddles of red brocade and its camel-trappings adorned with cowries and little bits of looking-glass, its gaily-striped awnings and brilliant tent linings.

With its crowds, too. Owen loved the bustle of the bazaars, of the whole native city, in fact; but after you had spent some time in them, especially when it was as hot as this, you felt an overwhelming need for space and air, and after forcing their way through the blocked thoroughfares of the Tentmakers' Bazaar they were glad to emerge into the more open streets. Mahmoud summoned an arabeah, one of the two-horse kind, and they sank into it gratefully.

Zeinab agreed that she would like a coffee and Mahmoud wanted to talk about what they had seen, so they stopped the arabeah when they reached the Ismailiya Quarter with its more Westernized restaurants into which women could go, and got out. It was late in the afternoon, almost evening by now, and the restaurants were beginning to fill up as people emerged from their siestas and began to promenade the streets. The shops took on a new lease of life, the street-sellers, with their lemonade and nougat, ostrich feathers, mummy-beads and scarabs, carnations and roses, and the street-artists, with their boa-constrictors and baboons, took new heart, and the city in general resumed its normal manic rhythm. They found a restaurant in a side street, where they would be pestered less, and took an outside table.

"Of the three, he's the most likely," said Mahmoud.

"Yes, but how certain are you that it's one of the three? How certain are you in the first place that it's a scentmaker?"

"Not at all," Mahmoud confessed.

"I mean, it's a brilliant deduction," said Owen, "but it's just a deduction."

"Just a deduction?" said Mahmoud, a little sharply.

"There isn't any real evidence."

"There is real evidence but not much of it. So you've got to use what there is. Hence deduction."

Owen was silent. He was tempted to ask if Mahmoud had learned that in college. Mahmoud, unlike Owen, had been trained for the job he was doing and sometimes reminded Owen of the fact. Owen did not like being reminded that he was, so far as police work was concerned, an amateur.

"Is there any corroborative evidence?" he asked.

He rather distrusted Gallic logic. Brilliant, yes, but was it sound? The Parquet lawyers, French-trained and French in style, had a name—among the English—for unreliability. Sometimes they homed in on the right conclusion with remarkable speed; sometimes they missed the point altogether.

"A bit," said Mahmoud. "Three other people noticed the woman. One of them remarked on the scent."

"Did they see her with the man?"

"Two of them did, including one who noticed the scent."

"Anyone get a good look at him?"

"No. None of them would be able to identify him. Except as a Copt, that is. They'd all noticed that."

"They would!"

"Yes. You'd prefer it not to be a Copt, wouldn't you?"

"Just at the moment I would."

"It's rather pointing that way, though."

"What else have you found out?"

"Nothing to link Zoser directly with the Zikr. One person thinks he saw him there. That was earlier in the evening, though."

"Have you checked whether he was in his shop?"

"Yes. He wasn't."

"Have you asked him why?"

"Haven't asked him anything yet. I was hoping for a positive identification. I don't suppose—?"

Owen shook his head.

"No," he said, "I didn't see him."

Mahmoud sighed.

"I was afraid of that," he said. "That leaves us with Miss Postlethwaite."

"That girl!" said Zeinab.

"Yes. You see," said Mahmoud, turning to her, "she was the only one who really saw them."

"Notices everything, doesn't she?"

"Yes," said Mahmoud enthusiastically. "She's an extraordinarily good observer."

Something must have told him that he'd not said quite the right thing, for he looked at Zeinab uneasily afterwards. Mahmoud stood a little in awe of Zeinab. It was partly her social position, partly her father, the formidable Nuri Pasha. Mahmoud detested everything that Nuri stood for: the old, near-feudal Egypt, with its hereditary great landlords, of whom Nuri was one; court-based politics, in which Nuri was adept; the power of the old order to block and frustrate all attempts at reform. But although he looked down on Nuri he also looked up at him, and because of that Nuri had a unique ability to touch Mahmoud on the raw. Something of all that had rubbed off on Zeinab, although Zeinab was Nuri's daughter only by a slave girl, a well-known courtesan, who had had mind enough of her own to refuse to join Nuri's harem. That was another thing which made Mahmoud uneasy, for modern and emancipated though he was, he could not completely shake off the attitudes and sexual constraints of the old, Islamic society. He even felt slightly awkward sitting out with her in a public place having coffee.

Zeinab added to his unease by opening her handbag, taking out the three small bottles of perfume and dropping them deliberately on the floor. She summoned a waiter to clear them away.

"Presumably you've done some background checking?" said Owen.

Mahmoud turned back to him with relief.

"Yes," he said. "I had my people check out the three scentmakers. One of them, the first one we saw, I think we can rule out straight away. He's not very strong physically, suffers from some sort of debilitating illness, hardly ever goes out. The fat one doesn't go out much either but in principle we can't rule him out. The third one could do it physically and gets out far more. He's very active in his local church, attends services there at all hours, mortifies himself, fasts, that sort of thing."

"A zealot?"

"Devout." Like Nikos, Mahmoud did not wish to be pushed into too firm religious characterization.

"Politically active?" Owen pressed.

"Not so far as I am aware."

"I'm looking for motive."

"That's the problem. I can't find one. That applies to them all. As far as I can tell, they have all three led blameless lives, had no criminal connection, kept themselves to themselves and as separate from Moslems as they could, and had no occasion to even meet a Zikr, let alone enter into a relationship with one which might lead them to want to kill him. They, and Zoser particularly, don't seem to have had much personal life at all."

"They sound very dull," said Zeinab.

"What church does he go to?" asked Owen. "Zoser, I mean. You said he went to a local church."

"The Mar Girgis—Church of St. George."

"By the Tunisian Bazaar?"

"Yes. You know it?"

"I know someone who goes to it," said Owen.

Mahmoud shrugged.

"Nothing special about it. Very Orthodox, a bit fundamentalist. Zoser's quite well known there. He's not one of the elders, he's not rich enough for that, or educated enough. He's just there at all the services."

"With his wife?"

"With his wife." He looked at Owen. "I was wondering—" he said tentatively.

"Yes?" said Owen.

"What were you wondering?" asked Zeinab.

"If you would like to go to church next Sunday," Mahmoud said, looking at Owen, "with Miss Postlethwaite."

"Why her?" asked Zeinab.

"She's the only one who could make a positive identification," Mahmoud explained. "She's important."

"I can see that," said Zeinab.

"It would be difficult in a church," said Owen. "The women are kept separate from the men."

"She could see him, though he wouldn't be able to see her. That might be an advantage."

"Why do *you* have to go?" Zeinab asked Owen.

"She would have to be escorted," said Mahmoud.

"Couldn't you do that?"

No, Mahmoud couldn't. He knew that and so did she. It would have to be a white man, an Englishman preferably. Zeinab knew that perfectly well. She was just trying to be awkward. And she was succeeding as far as Mahmoud was concerned. He flushed and his face went a little stiff.

"I am afraid it would have to be Captain Owen," he said.

"Very well," said Owen. "I'll ask her."

Zeinab rose from the table in a fury and flounced out.

"What have I done?" asked Mahmoud, bewildered and uncomfortable.

"It's nothing," said Owen, wondering whether he should follow her. It looked a bit silly if you followed a woman around like a lap-dog. On the other hand there would be trouble tonight if he didn't. He decided to strike a balance. He stayed at the table talking with Mahmoud for another moment or two and then went out into the street. Zeinab was nowhere to be seen.

From the far end of the corridor came the sound of angry dispute. After a while Owen could stand it no longer and went along.

"What the hell's going on?"

Outside the door, where the orderlies sat on the ground in a row, their backs to the wall, a woman was berating the coffee orderly, Yussuf. When she saw Owen she stopped, abashed. Yussuf gave her a great push.

"Away with you, woman!" he shouted furiously. "You bring me shame."

The woman fired up again.

"Yours is the shame," she said. "Yours was the shame already."

Yussuf tried to urge her away but she resisted his efforts.

"You bring shame on your family," she called out, so that everyone could hear. Heads began popping out of windows. The other orderlies watched with delight.

Yussuf caught hold of her and propelled her towards the gate. At the last moment she twisted away from him and ran back towards the orderlies. Yussuf bore down on her in a fury. Afraid that he was going to hit her, Owen intervened.

"Enough of this!" he snapped. "Be quiet, woman!"

The woman fell silent, though she kept darting angry glances at Yussuf.

"Who is this woman?" Owen asked Yussuf. "Your wife?"

"My sister, effendi."

Owen remembered the boy in the Coptic Place of the Dead.

"I have met your son, I think." The woman looked startled, then pleased. Then worried.

"He is a good boy, effendi," she said hastily. "He runs a little wild but there is no harm in him."

"He is clever beyond his years."

The woman looked even more worried.

"But he means no harm, effendi," she insisted.

"He is a good boy," said Owen reassuringly. He turned to Yussuf, associating him with family merit. "And you have a good nephew, Yussuf. You must come and speak to me about him when he is older." The remark, with its suggestion of possible patronage at his command, soothed Yussuf's ruffled pride. It also impressed his sister, who quietened down and looked at him with new respect.

"What is all this about?" Owen addressed himself to Yussuf. When Yussuf made no reply, Owen turned to his sister. "What has brought you here?"

"I wanted him to speak to his wife," she said in a low voice.

"Indeed? And what about?"

"He has put her away. And now he expects me to clean and cook for him."

"Our mother is dead," said Yussuf, "and I have no woman in my house."

"I have my own to look after," she protested.

"That is true," said Owen. "She has her own to look after. Cannot you pay a woman to come in?"

"Why should I pay," asked Yussuf, "when I have a sister?"

"Why should your sister work for you," the woman retorted, "when you have a wife?"

"I have no wife."

"You had one last week."

"But I haven't one now!" Yussuf roared.

"What was the difference between you?" Owen asked.

Yussuf did not reply.

"Nothing worth losing a wife over," his sister said.

Yussuf turned on her in a fury.

"You be quiet, woman!" he shouted. "What do you know about it?"

"I know what all the world knows," his sister maintained stoutly, "and that is that Fatima has always been a true wife to you."

Owen was rather relieved to hear this. If she had been unfaithful it would have been tricky to intervene.

"Is her fault so bad that it cannot be overlooked?" he asked. "No doubt she already repents."

"You might not be so lucky next time," Yussuf's sister observed.

Yussuf glared at her.

"He won't find it so easy to get another wife," she said to Owen. "They all know what he is like."

Yussuf boiled over.

"I?" he shouted dramatically. "I? What about her? Is she not to blame? I have given her house, clothes, a good bed. I do not beat her. Much. I give her money—"

"No, you don't," his sister said. "That is why she is always onto you."

Yussuf raised his hand threateningly. His sister, a woman of spirit, squared up to him. One of the orderlies, in defiance of the Prophet, began to lay bets.

Owen stepped in.

"Be off with you!" he said to the woman sternly. "Take this up at another time."

He ushered her firmly towards the gate.

"I will speak to him," he said to her when they had got out of earshot, "and see if I cannot resolve this matter."

She went quietly enough. Owen admired her independence,

but felt that reconciliation was more likely to be achieved in her absence.

Georgiades had asked Owen to meet him at a donkey-vous beside the Ezbekiya Gardens.

Owen liked the Ezbekiya, though gardens it was not. What it was was a dirty patch of fenced-off sand with a few straggly trees and occasional tufts of scrawny grass. In a land where, with a little water, anything would grow, and private gardens were a blaze of bougainvillaea and oleander, Cairo's public gardens remained bits of desert, and the only colour in the Ezbekiya was provided once a week by the uniforms of the incredibly incompetent Egyptian regimental band. The Ezbekiya did indeed have its moments, in the very early morning when there were few people about and the big falcons sailed over it with their unexpectedly musical cries and the Egyptian doves cooed softly in the palm trees, but on the whole what Owen liked was the Ezbekiya's outside.

All round the gardens were railings. And all along the railings were open-air stands, shops, stalls, restaurants, street-artists and tradesmen. Everything the ordinary Egyptian needed was there. The barber sat on the railings while his customers stood patiently in front of him to have their heads shaved. The tailor hung his creations on the railings. The hat-sellers marked off their territory with towers of tarbooshes, all fitting one on top of the other. The whip-makers plaited their whips through the railings and hung them from the trees.

There were trees all round the Ezbekiya, most of them comparatively young. Circular spaces about a yard wide had been cut in the pavement to receive them. To guard their roots the spaces were covered with gratings except for a few inches round the trunk. In this hole the chestnut-seller lit his fire, and on the gratings he set out his pans of roasted chestnuts. At night the coffee-sellers and the men who sold cups of hot sago brought their wares too; and all through the day there were sweet-sellers and nougat-sellers and nut-sellers and lemonade-sellers and tea-sellers and pie-sellers and cake-sellers—everything the sweet-toothed Egyptian might be persuaded to spend his little money on. Around each stall there were usually people talking, and the place which attracted the most conversationalists, after, perhaps, the pavement restaurants, was the donkey-vous.

This was the donkey-boys' stand. The donkeys, the little white donkeys of Cairo, lay about in the road and on the pavement among the huge green stacks of berseem brought there for their dinner by forage camels. They were very rarely disturbed, at least by foreigners, since to hire a donkey cost a foreigner as much as a cab and pair of horses. But in their saddles of red brocade and their necklaces of silver thread with blue beads they looked very picturesque and the tourists loved to photograph them. For that, of course, they paid, and that, during the tourist season, was what the donkey-vous was all about. That, and conversation.

There was more than one donkey-vous in the Ezbekiya but Owen knew which one to make for. It was next to a postcard-seller, and to get to it you had to go past a row of very strange postcards stuck on the railings: views of Cairo, oleographs of Levantine saints, scenes of the Massacre of the Marmelukes and from the Great War of Independence, portraits of the Madonna and of St. Catherine, and, of course, hundreds of indecent photographs, very precise in some respects, strangely vague in others. At the end of the row, their backs turned to all these visual riches, was a ring of donkey-boys squatting on the ground. Among them was Georgiades.

He stood up when he saw Owen approaching.

"Here's my friend," he said to the donkey-boys. "I've got to go."

He shook hands with several of the boys and exchanged farewell salaams with others.

"I wouldn't mind a cup of something," he said to Owen, so that the donkey-boys could hear, "and perhaps a bite or two. Have we got time?"

"Sure," said Owen. "No hurry."

They went over to the nearby tea-stall and then, with their glasses of tea, drifted over to one of the trees where a chestnut-seller was just lighting his fire. Georgiades peered into his basket.

"These look good ones," he said to the man. "How about doing a handful for me and my friend?"

"It will take a moment or two," the man said, "but it will be well worth the wait."

Owen and Georgiades went a little way off and squatted down beneath the trees to wait. The sun had set and it was already quite dark in the gardens. Beneath the trees it was darker still.

As they sat there someone came up and, as was not unusual, joined them in their conversation. It was the boy they had talked to in the Coptic Place of the Dead, the one who had given them information—and kicked Georgiades on the shin.

"Kick me again," said Georgiades, keeping his voice at the gentle, conversational level, "and I will kick your balls so hard that they will fly out of your backside."

Even in the darkness Owen could see the boy's teeth flash white in a big grin.

"That was good, wasn't it?" he said with pride. "They didn't suspect a thing."

"It was good," said Georgiades, "at my expense. However, we need not pursue this now. Ali wanted us to meet here," he said to Owen, "so that we should not be seen by his little friends."

"Your name is Ali, is it?" Owen asked the boy.

"Yes, effendi."

"And your mother is Yussuf's sister."

"Yes, effendi," said the boy, pleased that Owen had remembered. Relationships were important in Egyptian society. They conferred obligations. If a man was lucky enough to get a job it was expected that he would use his position to find jobs for others in his family or village. But they were also a guarantee. When a misdemeanour was committed, it was not the offender alone who was shamed but his whole family.

"Well, Ali," said Owen, "you have helped us already and I am grateful. Help us again and you will not lose by it."

"Unless they find out."

"They will not find out."

The boy was silent.

"Where do you want to begin?" Georgiades asked Owen.

"Let us go back to the Place of the Dead. That night. You saw the men and you told us whose men they were. What about the man who took the dog into the tomb? Whose man was he?"

"The same."

"Are you sure?" asked Owen. "My friend"—he meant Georgiades—"he asked among the men and they say he was not one of them."

"That is so," said the boy.

"Then—"

"He follows the one I spoke of. But not him alone."

"He follows another too?"

"He is a Zikr."

Afterwards a lot of things fell into place. For the moment, though, Owen was so caught by surprise that he could only repeat foolishly: "A Zikr?"

"Yes. Do you not know the Zikr? They are dervishes who call upon the name of God. Also, sometimes, they dance."

"I know the Zikr," said Owen, recovering.

"Well, then. This man is a Zikr. But he goes to the holy one's mosque."

"Which mosque is that?"

"It is close to the Bab es Zuweyla."

"The blue one?"

"Yes. The blue one."

The Blue Mosque, which Owen had seen the previous day on his visit to the bazaars, was a dervish mosque, used almost exclusively by such as the Zikr.

"He dances, then," said Owen.

"Yes."

"Did he dance the other night?"

"I do not know. I expect so."

"If we brought you to where you could see the Zikr, could you pick him out for us?"

"It was dark when I saw him," said the boy unwillingly.

"We would bring you where you could not be seen. And we would pay you better than well."

"In that case," said the boy, "I will come."

"Do you think you will be able to pick him out?"

"I remember now," said Ali, "that although it was dark that night, there was also a little moon."

The chestnut-seller laid out the chestnuts on the grating to cool and then brought them over to Owen and Georgiades. Ali slipped back into the shadows. When they looked round, he had gone.

"Will you be able to find him again?"

"No," said Georgiades. "But the little bugger can always find me."

He cradled the chestnuts in his hands, enjoying the warmth.

"What was so special about him being a Zikr?"

"I've got something else on with the Zikr."

He told Georgiades about the killing.

"Sounds as if Mahmoud's got it sorted out," Georgiades said.

"Zoser, you mean?"

"Isn't it?"

"Almost certainly, yes," said Owen. "Still, it would be nice if it was someone else. Not a Copt."

"At least you've got him. That ought to keep the Moslems happy."

"What about the Copts?"

"They'll be happy too," said Georgiades, "if you get the Moslem who put the dog in Andrus's tomb."

"That's why I'm hoping Ali will be able to pick him out."

Georgiades skinned a chestnut and popped it into his mouth.

"Have you thought," he said, "that he might be the one who's not there to be picked out?"

CHAPTER 6

Owen had been to the Coptic Cathedral before but not to a Coptic church; so he was surprised to find that most of the congregation appeared to be on crutches. Closer inspection revealed that the crutches were in fact walking-sticks; and the need for such support soon became apparent. The service was interminably long and the congregation had to stand throughout.

The men, that was. The women were better provided for and were allowed to sit down. They were, however, segregated in a separate compartment off to the right and screened by a heavy grille, through which, nevertheless, some of the women contrived to allow themselves to be seen. The compartment gave only an oblique view of the altar, which perhaps accounted for the distinct murmur of conversation behind the grille.

Owen had borrowed the wife of a Coptic colleague as a companion for Jane Postlethwaite. The two were now inside the grille together and Mena Iskander had been given strict instructions to try to secure Miss Postlethwaite a seat from which she could see Zoser clearly and if possible his wife as well. A tall order, perhaps, though Mena Iskander was a lady of resource and intrigued by the whole situation. Fortunately, Zoser, who was the more important of the two, was also the most easily seeable.

He stood in the front row of the congregation immediately beneath one of the huge, heavily-ornamented lecterns, and during the readings his rapt, upturned face caught the light from the lectern's candles. Watching his total absorption in the service and the way in which he hung upon the holy words, Owen could not help feeling a moment of doubt. Had they made a mistake?

However, in his time in Egypt, and before that in India, he had met many men of real devotion who yet had done the most terrible things, often in the name of the religion they served. It might be that Zoser was another such.

Of course it was not certain either that Zoser had done it or that, if he had done it, he had done it for sectarian reasons. But it had all the signs of a sectarian killing. Mahmoud had been unable to uncover anything of a personal nature which might have prompted the attack. Indeed, so far he had not been able to discover any previous relationship at all between Zoser and the Zikr. And, unfortunately, sectarian attacks were not at all uncommon. Cairo was a city of many nationalities and many different systems of belief. There were large communities of Greeks, Armenians, Jews, Turks, Levantines, Italians, French and English, as well as the more indigenous Copts, Arabs, Berbers from the south and Negroes. And each community, Cairo being Cairo, had at least two rival sects. Owen found it hard to keep track of all of them. But keep track he had to, for the sects were always at odds with each other and sometimes their differences spilled over into killings. What one tended to get, too, was not just sect against sect, but a fundamentalist sect of one religion against a fundamentalist sect of another, Christian against Moslem, another Coptic sect against—Zikr?

A sudden crash of cymbals pulled him back to the present. At regular, but otherwise apparently arbitrary points during the service an acolyte would emerge from a recess, face the congregation and clash the cymbals violently together. Then he would retire. Owen suspected that it was to make sure that nobody fell asleep. There was some danger of this since hardly anyone present could understand a word. The service was conducted throughout in traditional Coptic, a language found only in churches and a few schools, and which very few even of the Copts understood. They habitually spoke Egyptian Arabic.

There was another mighty crash and a priest began walking through the congregation swinging a censer and laying his hand on the head of anyone who offered. Among those who offered was Zoser.

People began to stir and Owen got the impression that the service was approaching its end. The priest completed his circuit and disappeared behind the altar screen, leaving in his wake a long trail of incense which gradually mounted into the roof and lost itself among the ostrich eggs and silver censers suspended there. There was a final reading, mercifully brief, and a last clash of cymbals; and then from behind the altar screen came a procession of priests and acolytes and small boys holding lighted tapers and carrying a large picture. They paraded round the church showing the picture to all parts of the congregation. Then they, too, retreated behind the altar screen with a last puff of smoke and the chanting came to an end.

Outside, he joined up with Mahmoud and waited for the two women. They came up the steps with a Coptic woman in a long black gown and veil. As they stepped out into the sunshine Mena Iskander's reticule slipped and fell on the ground. She walked on without noticing. The Coptic woman hesitated, then picked up the reticule and hurried after Mena. Mena thanked her profusely, taking her impetuously by both hands. The woman's sleeves fell back and there was the hand-painting.

The ladies parted. The Coptic woman went to one side and stood waiting for her husband, who was delayed in the church. Mena and Jane came towards them.

"Brilliant!" said Owen.

"Mrs. Iskander," said Mahmoud, "you are remarkable!"

Mena Iskander looked bashfully at the ground. She was not used to receiving compliments from men in public.

"Did you see?" she asked.

Owen looked at Jane Postlethwaite. She nodded.

Zoser came hurrying out of the church and joined his wife. From under her huge hat and the light grey veil she had thoughtfully donned for the occasion Jane Postlethwaite regarded them steadily.

When they had returned Mena Iskander to her amused husband they went with Jane Postlethwaite back to her hotel, where Owen earned unmerited credit for his morning's occupation.

"Copts," said John Postlethwaite. "They would be a sort of Nonconformist here, would they?"

"Sort of," said Owen.

Paul, who had accompanied John Postlethwaite to an Anglican service, gave Owen an approving glance.

"That's more like it, Gareth. Keep it up. The Pyramids tomorrow. Yes? Please?"

Their credit was increased, in John Postlethwaite's eyes, when they ordered coffee. Most of the British in the hotel were drinking something stronger. Mahmoud, of course, as a Moslem, did not drink alcohol, and Owen, who habitually took on protective colouring, fell into line without thinking.

They took it on the terrace where there was more air and a slight breeze ruffled Jane Postlethwaite's sleeves.

"Get what you wanted?" Owen asked.

Mahmoud looked at Jane Postlethwaite.

"She had touched up her hands," said Jane Postlethwaite, "but the pattern was the same."

"It was the woman you saw?"

"Yes."

"You would be prepared to swear to that?"

"I would," said Jane Postlethwaite firmly.

"And Zoser?"

"He was the man I saw."

Mahmoud sat back with a little sigh of relief.

"Thank you, Miss Postlethwaite," he said. "There was always the chance that you might not."

Jane Postlethwaite sipped her coffee meditatively.

"When so much depends upon it," she said, "it seems wrong to be so certain."

"But if you were certain—?"

"I know," she said, "I should say so. Well, I am prepared to say so."

"A man's life was taken," Mahmoud pointed out.

"Yes. That is why I am prepared to testify."

Owen felt that things were moving a little too fast.

"That may not be necessary, Miss Postlethwaite," he said smoothly.

The British community would not be very happy about the involvement of one of its ladies in a public trial. Nor, it occurred to him, in the special circumstances of John Postlethwaite's visit, was the Consul-General likely to be overjoyed.

Jane Postlethwaite looked puzzled.

"Don't you want me to give evidence?" she demanded.

"Well, it's not quite that—"

"Yes," said Mahmoud.

Jane Postlethwaite looked uncertainly from one to the other.

"It may prove distressing for you, Miss Postlethwaite," said Owen.

"And you would like to spare me?"

"Of course."

Jane Postlethwaite looked down into her lap. Then she raised her head.

"Captain Owen," she said, "do you think that proper?"

"Well . . ."

"When so much is at stake?"

"Well . . ."

"Captain Owen, why do you wish to spare me?"

"Because . . . because . . ." he fumbled.

"Because I am a pretty girl?"

There was no answer to that one.

"Or because I am British?"

"Both."

Jane Postlethwaite rose from the table in a fury.

"That is not right, Captain Owen," she said icily. "That is not right."

As she reached the door, she turned.

"If you wish me to give evidence, Mr. el-Zaki," she said, "I certainly shall."

"Sorry!" said Mahmoud.

"Christ!" said Owen.

They walked a little way in silence. It was the hottest part of the day, and apart from them there was nothing moving in the streets. Even the donkeys were lying down.

"It's not much," said Mahmoud.

"Not much?"

Mahmoud, however, was thinking of the case.

"It's not much to go on. A positive identification, yes, but only by one person."

Owen allowed his mind to drain back.

"Any corroborative evidence?"

"Hardly," Mahmoud admitted.

"It's not strong," said Owen.

That was another thing; if it was Jane Postlethwaite's word against Zoser's, the court would almost certainly convict. But it would look bad. The word of a European against the word of an Egyptian. It would be OK if there was other evidence. But to convict on her word alone! The Nationalist papers would pick it up. They might make quite a thing of it. They'd do it deliberately to embarrass the Government. And, my God, they would certainly succeed if it came out that she was Postlethwaite's niece.

"I thought you wanted to wrap it up quickly," said Mahmoud in injured tones.

"I do," said Owen. "But it's got to be watertight. Suppose we don't clinch it? The Copts will say we tried to put it on him and the Moslems will say we let him off."

"I could always pull him in for questioning."

"Think he'd talk?"

"They sometimes do."

Sectarian killers especially. They usually didn't even bother to deny the charge. They saw it, rather, as something to boast of.

"Think he would?"

Mahmoud was silent.

"No," he said. "Not unless I could shake him."

"And for that you need something to shake him with. Are your men going to come up with anything?"

"At the moment," said Mahmoud, "there doesn't seem to be a lot for them to come up with."

"No previous contact?"

"Apparently not. Zoser keeps himself pretty much to himself. All his contacts seem to be within the Coptic community. Apart from work. And that doesn't help us much because, so far as we have been able to ascertain, the Zikr doesn't appear to have bought a bottle of perfume in his life."

"It's not the sort of thing he would buy, is it?"

"No, he's not that sort. And that's another thing. The two men are as different as chalk and cheese. It's hard to see how they could ever get to know each other long enough for it to come to this. Zoser's withdrawn, doesn't have much to do with people. Religion is everything to him. The Zikr must have been devout too, of course, but he got round a lot more than Zoser, mixed with people, liked crowd and noise and a bit of fun. Something of a character, too. People say he was a bit of a joker."

"A joker?"

The idea came to him. Or came back to him. Something that Georgiades had said.

"I know," said Mahmoud. "It's hard to imagine a Zikr being a bit of a joker, isn't it? Still, they can't always be chanting and dancing. They've got lives of their own too."

"It's not that."

"No? Well, anyway, my men have been unable to find any connection between the two at all. Which almost certainly makes it a sectarian killing."

"Yes," said Owen, "but why him? Him particularly?"

Mahmoud shrugged.

"He was the nearest?" he suggested.

"But he wasn't, was he? Zoser picked him out."

"We don't know that."

"OK. Put it another way: what made Zoser start picking?"

"He doesn't like Moslems."

"Yes. But what made him decide to do something about it? Now?"

"It suddenly came over him?"

"Something triggered it off. What was that something?"

"I don't know. Do you?"

"I might," said Owen. "I might."

"What the hell's this?" said Georgiades, staring into his mug unbelievingly.

"Yussuf's got problems," said Nikos from his desk.

"I'm going to speak to him," said Owen.

"For God's sake speak to him quickly," said Georgiades. "Otherwise I'll have problems."

"I've got one for you already," said Owen.

"Thank you."

"The problem is this: how do we find out whether the Zikr who put the dog in Andrus's tomb is also the Zikr who got killed?"

"I see your problem," said Georgiades, after a moment's reflection.

"Get that boy to have a look at the body," said Nikos.

"He's only a child," Owen objected.

Nikos shrugged his shoulders and went on with his writing.

"Look," said Georgiades. "I hate to shatter these gentle English illusions—"

"Welsh," said Owen.

"That's right," said Georgiades, "somewhere over there. But that innocent child earns his livelihood robbing corpses."

"Bloody hell!" said Owen.

Nikos looked up.

"What else do you expect him to do?" he asked. "He's living in the graveyard, isn't he?"

"Yes, but—"

"It's not much of a living. Everybody knows about it so they don't leave anything valuable on the body."

"Except Copts," said Nikos.

"He robs Moslems too," said Georgiades. "No sectarian prejudice here. No," he said, turning to Owen, "that's not the problem."

"What is?"

"Where's the body?"

Owen thought for a moment.

"I'd assumed it was in the mortuary. Either still at the lab or somewhere else."

Georgiades shook his head.

"No. Too crowded. They need the space."

"You mean it's been handed back already?"

"They don't keep them for long."

"If you just rush down now," said Nikos, "you can interrupt a Moslem funeral and desecrate that too."

"I didn't desecrate it."

"You could always take a dog."

"Shut up. What are we going to do?" he appealed to Georgiades.

"Find out where the body is. If it's in any of the mortuaries, OK. If it's been handed back I'll find out where the tomb is. They always bring them the same day so there's not much point in looking anywhere else. Anyway, there would be too many people around."

The implications of what Georgiades was saying sank in.

"Break into the tomb? Christ!"

"There's no other way."

"Yes, I know. But—"

"Look," said Georgiades patiently, "do you want this settled or don't you? Is it important? If it's not, well, I'm not exactly keen. But if it might stop a massacre . . ."

"It might stop a massacre."

"OK, then."

Owen was still not happy.

"Suppose we were seen?"

"You will be seen," said Nikos.

"Yes," said Georgiades. "Those little bastards."

He rubbed his chin.

"I've got an idea," he said. "Why don't I have a word with that little sod Ali and see if he can arrange it all? It would need money but it would be worth it. If he's seen, or they are seen, that's OK. There's nothing out of the ordinary. Whereas if we're seen it'll start a Holy War."

"You won't be able to use his evidence," said Nikos. "Not in court."

"We wouldn't anyway."

"Why do it, then?"

"It sets his mind at rest," said Georgiades, looking at Owen.

"It would give a motive," said Owen, "and once you've got that, you've got other lines to work on."

"All right," said Nikos.

"Can you trust Ali?" asked Owen.

"No," said Georgiades, "but you can trust money."

"I mean afterwards. Is he going to talk?"

"I don't think he'll talk," said Georgiades. "His mates may."

"We wouldn't want it to get out."

"I'll speak to Ali."

"It's risky."

"Got any better suggestions?"

"No," said Owen regretfully.

"Want me to get on with it, then?"

"Yes."

As Georgiades went out, Nikos said: "At least it will bring the Copts and the Moslems together."

"What?"

"When they find out it's the Greeks that are breaking into their tombs."

Owen was pursuing Garvin about the Camel Watering Account.

"It's damned silly," he said. "We always need money at this time of year. And we always transfer it out of the Camel Watering Account. Why the hell can't we do it this year?"

"Because they're looking, that's why. Usually they don't bother. They've got other things to think about."

"And this year they haven't?"

"This year they've got Postlethwaite looking over their shoulder so they're making damned sure they're being strictly kosher."

"I don't mind them playing their little games," Owen complained. "It's just that they have real effects. On me. It affects my work."

"Does it?" said Garvin, not really very interested.

"Yes, it does. I rely on it to supplement the Curbash Compensation Fund."

"What?"

"Curbash Compensation Fund. It's what I pay the bribes out of."

"The curbash was abolished years ago."

One of Cromer's first acts had been to abolish the use by government officials of the *curbash,* the whip, as a means of enforcing obedience.

"I know, but the fund still exists. When the curbash was abolished they set it up to compensate anyone who was whipped after the abolition. You see, they couldn't rely on the local beys not to forget it had been abolished. So they set up this fund to compensate victims in serious cases of abuse. They didn't want to make too much fuss about it, otherwise the whole population would come along claiming they'd been whipped. So the fund's administered by the Mamur Zapt."

"Have there been any claims?"

"Not recently."

"And there's a grant each year?"

"That's right. That's what makes it so convenient. The trouble is, we've been having to spend more money on bribes lately. It's never enough. So," concluded Owen, "I have to transfer money from the Camel Watering Account."

"Otherwise you'll have to cut back on bribes?"

"Yes."

Garvin toyed with the ebony paperweight on his desk.

"Yes," he said, "I see your point."

He thought for a moment or two.

"Can't you use some other account?"

"No. It's nearly the end of the financial year and most of the money's been spent. Anyway, why the hell should I? The system's worked all right up to now. The Consul-General wants the work done, doesn't he?"

"Yes, but he doesn't want to know about it. And above all he doesn't want to see it appearing in the accounts. They are scrutinized, you know, by a parliamentary committee back at home. How do you think it would look if there was a Mamur

Zapt Bribes Account? All the little Postlethwaites would go berserk."

"We don't have to call it that. 'Special Purposes' or something like that."

"Create something new in finance," said Garvin, "a new code, a new sub-heading, and that 's always the thing that gets picked out. Stick to what they're familiar with."

"OK," said Owen. "I'll stick to the Curbash Compensation Fund. But I still want some more money in it."

"That's what they all say. Including the Khedive. He wants his allocation upped too."

"It's his money, isn't it?"

"No. It's ours. He doesn't have a bean, other than what we lend him. That's why we're here."

Of all the countries in the world, Egypt was perhaps the most thoroughly in debt. Its international indebtedness had reached such alarming proportions under the previous Khedive that its Western creditors had become seriously alarmed. Britain, as the largest of these, had stepped in to sort out the country's chaotic finances. But that had been thirty years before, and the British were still there. Egypt's finances, they claimed, were still unsettled.

"Besides," said Garvin, "all he wants it for is to go to Monte Carlo again. So we're not keen."

"But my money—" Owen began.

"Is part of it. He wants a larger allocation in any case. That means more taxes. And here there's potentially big trouble, because the way he wants to do that is by taxing the Copts more."

"Just them?"

"Just them."

"They won't be pleased."

"They're not pleased."

"I've not heard anything about this."

"You wouldn't have. It's still being fought out inside the ministry. Finance are resisting it strongly. No wonder. They're all Copts."

"If this gets out—"

"Yes. You'll be busy, won't you?"

"I'll need more money."

Garvin shook his head.

"No chance. There's a veto across the board on any increase. Until the main thing gets settled."

"What do I do, then?"

"You'll have to use the resources you've got," said Garvin, and smiled ambiguously.

"Well," said Georgiades, "I've found out what you wanted."

He came into the room and poured himself a glass of water from the earthenware jug which stood, as it did in all the offices of Cairo, in the window so that the air currents could cool it. Although it was very hot, Owen had not put the fan on. It was a huge, three-bladed affair suspended from the roof and when it was at full blast it was hard to keep papers still on his desk.

"It was the Zikr?"

"The man who put the dog in Andrus's tomb and the man who got stabbed are one and the same Zikr."

"You're sure?"

"Ali is sure."

"I'm not going to ask you how he made sure."

"It cost a lot of money."

Owen winced.

"He had to do deals. Each of these gangs have got their own territory. Ali's territory is the Coptic graveyard so he had to make arrangements with the gangs in the Moslem graveyard. It's a big one and there are three gangs involved."

"The more people in it, the more it's likely to get out."

"If anything get out," said Georgiades, "it won't be linked with us."

"I hope so. I certainly hope so."

Georgiades put the glass down and mopped his brow. He was a bulky man and had been walking the streets and the sweat was running off him.

"What are you going to do now?"

"It gives us a motive, doesn't it?"

"Does it?"

"That's why Zoser killed him."

"Why should Zoser care? It's not his tomb."

"Zoser doesn't think like that. For him it's a religious matter. It was an affront to his God."

"Which he decided to avenge?"

"Yes."

"All by himself?"

"Why not?"

"He's only a little man," said Georgiades, eyeing the glass again. He made up his mind and poured out some more water.

"Are you saying you think someone put him up to it?" Owen demanded.

"What do you think?"

"I think," said Owen, "that at least we've got bloody Zoser. That'll satisfy the Moslems. And the Copts are hardly in a position to complain. We could look for the people who put him up to it. In fact, we might well do that. Quietly. No hurry. But we don't have to."

"You'd prefer to see it ended?"

"Yes."

"OK." Georgiades finished the glass and put it down.

"As long as everybody else sees it the same way," he said.

"I can't use this?" said Mahmoud.

"You can use it," said Owen, "but not in court. My informant is not in a position to testify."

"A pity. There's no chance you could persuade him?"

"No chance at all."

"What about the first identification? The Zikr who planted the dog?"

"That too."

"Pity. You see, if I had the original identification I could at least match it up against a description."

"Afraid not."

"The same informant?"

"The same informant."

"You're relying on him a lot."

"I think he's pretty reliable."

"But he won't talk? In public, I mean?"

"That's right."

"Well," said Mahmoud, "it's something, at any rate. Now that I know what I'm looking for I'll see if I can dig it out by other means."

"Are you going to pull him in?"

"Not till I've done some more checking. I'd like to have a bit more before I go for him."

"Don't leave it too long. Otherwise he mightn't be there when you go to pick him up."

And that was the trouble. For when, two days later, Mahmoud's men went to call on Zoser, they found that the bird had flown.

CHAPTER 7

"Didn't you ever have a man on him?" said Owen incredulously.

Mahmoud flushed.

"I don't have as many men as you," he replied angrily.

"Even so!"

Owen was furious. He had counted on wrapping this up. With Zoser inside, at least he would have headed off trouble from the Moslems. Now he couldn't count on that. And suppose they found out that a man had slipped through their fingers? It would be even worse. Mahmoud had bungled it. Not to pick Zoser up was fair enough, he had advocated that himself. But not to put a man on him. That was bloody stupid.

In fact, Mahmoud had put a man on Zoser but he preferred not to admit it. The man had gone to sleep, or at least that was what Mahmoud suspected, and that, to Mahmoud, was an even harder thing to admit than that he had not posted a man in the first place. Not being able to post a man was a matter of economics. Having one go to sleep on the job, well, that was just incompetence; and Mahmoud was very sensitive to the charge of Egyptian incompetence. Especially as, privately, he thought the charge was often justified.

It was in a case like this, too, that the weakness of the Egyptian system became apparent. The Parquet, the Department of Prosecution of the Ministry of Justice, which Mahmoud belonged to, and the Police were two entirely different and separate organizations. Mahmoud was responsible for collecting the evidence, deciding whether there was a case, and then carrying through prosecution. In doing so he had to rely on the police for manpower. Working to his instructions, they would collect evidence, do low-level questioning, keep people under surveillance, and if necessary arrest. The trouble was that since they were not directly under his control he was unable to ensure the quality of their work in the way that, for example, Owen could. What made matters worse was that the police were so badly paid that they could be recruited only from poor, country districts and lacked the sophistication, education and even, Mahmoud suspected at times, mother-wit of city people. Owen, because he could pay more, was able to draw his own men almost exclusively from the city. That was another thing that Mahmoud felt was wrong.

Owen's reaction touched him on a sore spot; and it was made all the sorer by an angry feeling inside him that there had indeed been incompetence, Egyptian incompetence, that he, Mahmoud, was ultimately responsible for it—and that there was absolutely nothing that he could in practice do about it.

"There must have been a leak," he said sullenly.

Owen was taken aback. This was something that had not occurred to him.

"A tip-off?"

"Yes. How else would he have known?"

"The church? The visit to the Scentmakers' Bazaar? Your men's inquiries?"

This upset Mahmoud still further. His men again.

"Their inquiries were general," he said harshly. "They are always making such inquiries. There was nothing to link them directly to Zoser."

"Surely they asked questions about Zoser?"

"And others."

"That might have been enough. Or maybe, seeing us the second time, he might have suspected. Especially if he spotted that it was the third time, for Miss Postlethwaite and me."

Mahmoud was silent.

"How much notice did you give your men?"

Mahmoud was now in one of those moods in which he found implied criticism hard to take. Owen half-realized this and if he had had any sense would have shut up, but Mahmoud's moods blew up very suddenly out of an apparently clear sky and once again he was slow in reacting.

"They had no notice."

Mahmoud did not say that this was because he did not trust them. "I made up my mind, collected them and went straight down."

"Anyone else in your office know?"

"No. Anyway," said Mahmoud, "I don't have any Copts in my office. What about you?"

Nikos. Owen pushed the thought immediately aside.

"If I did," he said, "they are people I can trust."

"Are you sure?"

"Yes," said Owen. "I am quite sure."

Mahmoud shrugged. The gesture came across offensively. In some way it conveyed utter disbelief.

Owen boiled over.

"Well," he said, "now that you've lost him, you'd better find him."

The way he put it made it sound like an order. Mahmoud turned on his heel and went off without a further word.

"Well," said Georgiades, "he could be right, couldn't he?"

"No," said Owen, "he couldn't."

Georgiades spread his hands. Owen distrusted these Cairene gestures of openness.

"Look at it this way: two loyalties. One to you, one to his people. Both real, both genuine. If he can serve one without hurting the other too much, what the harm?"

"It would hurt me. It would hurt the department."

"How much?"

"It hits at the work we do."

"How much? Just this one instance?"

"It's his people I'm trying to help."

"And the Moslems."

"I'm neutral."

"He's not."

"He's neutral when he works for me."

"Mostly. Mostly."

"Are you saying that in this case he's playing a game of his own?"

"I'm only saying that he might be."

Owen was silent. Before transferring to the Egyptian service he had been a regular-army officer in India and at times his military background reasserted itself. He liked things, or at least people, or at least those people near him, to be straightforward. He found it hard, almost impossible, to accept any deceit on Nikos's part. Internally, that was. So far as the rest of the world was concerned he could conceive of almost any deception. But among themselves . . .

"It's only a hypothesis," he said.

"Sure!" Georgiades agreed quickly. "Sure."

"You don't know anything that makes it anything more?"

"No, I'm just figuring out all the angles."

"It could be someone else."

"It needn't even be in this office."

"OK, then."

"If I were you," said Georgiades, "I'd forget about it. Only . . ."

"Only what?"

"Be careful."

Owen knew what he meant. While they were working on this case there were some things which Nikos had better not know.

"OK."

Georgiades smiled cheerfully. He had just suggested that his closest colleague might be, in this at least, a traitor. But there was nothing personal in it. Nikos was still his friend. Georgiades still trusted him. As much as he trusted anybody.

Owen was going through the accounts with Nikos trying to find pockets of money which might still be emptied. They came to the end of one set. While Nikos was collecting the papers Owen said casually:

"When they went to find Zoser, he wasn't at home."

Nikos understood immediately.

"A tip-off?"

"It looks like it."

Nikos's mind began automatically to turn over the possibilities, as it always did.

"That's funny," he said.

"Why?"

"Zoser doesn't strike me as the sort of person who would have contacts."

"Maybe it was just a sympathizer."

Nikos nodded.

"Yes. Perhaps you'd better review all Copts working in the office. Including me. Do the same with Mahmoud's office."

Owen did not say anything.

Nikos's thoughts moved on to a different tack.

"He doesn't have many friends. And they're all Copts. He must be in one of the Coptic parts of the city."

"And there are plenty of those."

"Mahmoud will be checking his friends," said Nikos. "That's obvious."

He frowned for a moment in concentration.

"The centre of Zoser's life is the church," he said. "I'll get you a list of the people who go there regularly."

"Do you think you'll be able to?"

Nikos looked at him with scorn, scooped up the remaining papers and went out.

It was the old, normal Nikos. Owen was a hundred per cent sure that he was OK.

Well, ninety-nine per cent.

Owen had other fish to fry and for the next two days he was busy on other things. He kept his men off the case, too. Mahmoud would be going over Zoser's contacts with a fine-tooth comb and, especially after their last exchange, Owen did not want to queer his pitch.

There were developments, however. He was sitting at his desk on the second morning when Nikos stuck his head through the door.

"Here they are again," he said.

"They" were the assistant kadi and the two sheikhs who had been before. This time it was the kadi who did most of the talking.

"It's about that murder," he said. "My friends are concerned that nothing seems to be happening."

"Oh, a lot is happening," Owen assured him. "It's just that we need to be absolutely sure before proceeding. Especially in a case like this."

"Not 'absolutely sure,' " said the kadi legalistically. " 'Reasonably certain' will do."

"Reasonably certain, then," Owen amended.

"And you are not in that position yet?"

"Pretty nearly, I would say. Of course, the case is in the hands of the Parquet."

"It is just that my friends are coming under great pressure from their communities over the incident."

The two sheikhs nodded in unison.

"I am sorry that should be so," said Owen. "I can assure them that we are making every effort. And, as I said, I think that we shall shortly be in a position to proceed against someone."

"Rumour has it," said the kadi, "that the Parquet sought to arrest someone and were unsuccessful."

"I'm afraid you'll have to ask the Parquet about that."

"The trouble is," said the kadi, "that apparently the man was a Copt. That makes it especially difficult for my friends. You see, there is word in the bazaar that perhaps the man heard beforehand that the Parquet were coming. And the communities are asking whether that was, perhaps, because he was a Copt."

"On that at least I can set your friends' minds at rest. Whether the man was Copt or Moslem would make no difference."

"So there was a man?"

"I was speaking hypothetically. If there was a man, it would make no difference whether he was Copt or Moslem. The Mamur Zapt is even-handed."

The two sheikhs looked a little perturbed. One of them tried to say something. The kadi affected not to notice and went smoothly on.

"I am sure of that," he said. "The doubt was rather about the impartiality of the offices. There are a lot of Copts in them."

"I am sure they are loyal and honest servants of the Khedive."

"I hope so. But things like this make one doubt, don't you think?"

Owen judged it best to make no reply. He just smiled winningly.

The sheikh, now, would not be restrained.

"This is a bad man," he said, "and he must be punished."

"He will be. Of that I can assure you."

"My people are angry. They say that the Government is not even-handed."

"Tell your people that the Government seeks to stamp out wrongdoing wherever it is found."

"We have told them that," said the other sheikh unexpectedly, "but they will not listen to us."

"My friends are coming under great pressure," said the kadi.

"I appreciate that. And I will do what I can. But one must not hasten justice at the expense of justice."

"True." The sheikhs nodded agreement.

"But," one of them said, "it is important that no one who has done wrong should escape justice."

"I will see," said Owen, "that he doesn't."

The sheikhs suddenly looked satisfied. Owen realized that was what they had come for. The personal assurance of the Mamur Zapt. In a society that was still traditional and oral, personal promises counted for a lot. In a way it was flattering that they should take his word. However, he knew that if he failed to live up to it they would not take his word again.

The kadi rose to his feet.

"Thank you for seeing us. My friends are very anxious that there should be no difference between their people and the Mamur Zapt, and will do all they can to see that things go no further, at least for the time being. Unfortunately"—he caught Owen's eye meaningfully—"they cannot answer for others."

With the usual extended Arabic farewells, the party was shown out. Owen accompanied them to the front entrance himself. He wanted to keep Nikos in the background.

The two sheikhs managed to keep control in their communities but in other ones there were disturbing incidents. Shops owned by Copts were attacked and wrecked and there were increasing instances of individual Copts being set upon in the streets. Zeinab became involved in one of these.

She frequently made use of Coptic craftsmen and one of them, a leather-worker, who had been repairing a handbag she was particularly fond of, was bringing it to her flat with his small son when he was attacked by a gang of youths. The boy ran on to the flats where Zeinab lived and rushed in at the entrance. Two of his attackers followed him and caught him and were about to drag him back out into the street when Zeinab came down the stairs. Zeinab had no great love of Copts but she wasn't having anyone attacked in the entrance of her building and pitched into the youths with such fury that they ran off.

The boy, weeping and bleeding, recognized Zeinab as the lady they were coming to see and managed to stammer out the story of the attack on his father. Zeinab, who tended to see things in personal terms and who, having been brought up in her father's house, had something of the great lady in her, took it into her head to protect her servants and rushed out into the street in a passion. She came upon the leather-worker further along the street surrounded by a mob of youths who were beating and kicking him.

Without thinking, she plunged into the mob, caught hold of the leather-worker and tried to drag him away from his assailants. The youths, being Moslems, were not having this from any woman, even if she were a great lady, and things would have gone ill for Zeinab if Owen had not arrived at that moment, on his way to her flat.

He caught hold of the two nearest him and knocked their heads together, kicked two more and grabbed the ringleaders. The others, thinking there was more of him, fled. Fortunately, none of them were armed. If they had been, it might have been a different story, for Owen himself only carried arms when he had reason to believe he might need them.

He put a neck-lock on the youth he was holding and looked around for help.

Now the fighting was over there was plenty forthcoming. He got some of the men to carry the leather-worker to Zeinab's flat. Others went to fetch a policeman. When, some time later, one appeared, Owen handed the youth over to him with strict instructions to keep him in the local caracol until Owen would question him. Then he went to Zeinab's flat.

Zeinab was sponging the boy's face. His father had already been attended to and lay quiet and grateful on one of Zeinab's sofas.

"You're going to have to do something about this," said Zeinab, looking up at him.

The caracol, one of the old ones, consisted of a single room underground. It was hot and foetid in there and Owen had the ringleader brought upstairs for questioning.

The boy was about fourteen years old and had the long, fuzzy hair of the dervish. He looked scared, not so much, Owen judged, because he was in the hands of the police but rather because he was in different surroundings from those he was used to, the modern, built-up, Europeanized part of the city and not the warren of tiny mediaeval streets he normally inhabited.

Owen sat on a chair in the cramped little office and made the boy stand in front of him.

"What is your name?" he asked.

"Daouad."

"Where are you from?"

"I am from near the Sukkariya," the boy growled.

"Well, Daouad, you will not see the Sukkariya again for a long time unless you answer my questions."

The boy looked around like a trapped animal.

"Whose man are you?"

"I am no man's man."

"You come from the Sukkariya. You are a dervish. Who is your sheikh?"

"The Sheikh Osman Rahman," the boy said reluctantly.

"Did he tell you to do this?"

The boy was silent.

"Will he be angry if I tell him what you have done?"

"No," said the boy proudly. "He will be pleased."

"Because you have done his bidding?"

"Because I have done what he wants."

"How do you know it is what he wants?"

The boy would not say. After a moment, though, he looked away and muttered: "It was only a pig of a Copt."

"There are always Copts. Why attack one now?"

"To avenge!" the boy said hotly. "To avenge the blow against one of ours! A death for a death!"

"Is that what the sheikh says?"

"It is what we all say."

"There are other sheikhs who do not say it."

"They turn the cheek," the boy said, "when they should set their face in anger. They fold their arms when they should lift their hand in wrath. They let the faithless strike them when they should strike the faithless."

The words had the ring of preacher's rhetoric.

"Is that what the Sheikh Osman says?"

"Yes," said the boy defiantly.

Owen had him taken back to the underground room. In a few days he would release him. There was no point in acting against him.

The Sheikh Osman Rahman, however, was a different matter.

Owen came up with him that evening. It was in a tiny square of the Old City. There was a dais on one side of the square on which the Sheikh Osman sat cross-legged. All around him, squatting on the ground, were his followers; and beyond them, around the outskirts and blocking up the mouths of the little streets which gave on to the square, was a wider, more disinterested audience. Those nearest the dais carried raised torches in their hands, so that the dais was illuminated and the sheikh clearly visible to all.

Owen stayed in one of the side streets and listened. The sheikh was only just getting into his stride. He spoke vehemently but quietly. He was expounding a *sura,* one of the parable-like stories of the Koran, extracting from it lessons for the faithful. As he pointed up the moral, contrasting the way of the good with the way of the bad, his voice deepened and became more indignant. Almost imperceptibly the exposition became a harangue. The crowd stirred and became involved. There were sympathetic cries. The sheikh now had moved into denunciation: of the wrongdoer, the infidel, those who mocked Islam. Of those who protected the infidel from the just wrath of the servants of Allah.

Owen waited for the words which would justify his own intervention. They came. Incitation to riot. His men, who knew the law as well as he, looked at him expectantly.

"Not yet."

He did not want to do it in front of the crowd. That might provoke a riot, the very thing he was trying to avoid. He did sometimes break up meetings but that was usually when they were political. Religion you handled with kid gloves.

Afterwards. When the crowd was beginning to disperse.

He could sense his men fidgeting. This was always the difficult time. They were disciplined, though, Sudanis, hand-picked ex-soldiers from the south. They would do what they were told.

The sheikh began a final exhortation. The last part of his *serman,* or speech was accompanied by continuous cries from his followers. His voice rose to a howl and drew the audience up with it into an excited, almost exalted, crescendo.

And then it stopped. The shouting went on, though, for several minutes. People leapt to their feet and milled around excitedly. This was the moment when, sometimes, a procession formed and they would march off to take action. If they did on this occasion Owen would be ready. His men drew their truncheons.

For a moment or two it seemed as if that was what would happen. A little group of men had got together and appeared to be trying to enlist others into a formation of some kind. There was so much untidy milling about, however, that in the confines of the tiny space they found it hard to organize themselves and eventually seemed to abandon the attempt.

The excitement died away and the crowd began to drift off down the side streets. The throng in front of Owen melted away, leaving his men exposed, so he drew them back into the shadows. In the square the torches began to go out, until there were only one or two left near the dais.

The Sheikh Osman sat on, relaxed now. A few of his followers had joined him on the dais.

Then he, too, rose to his feet. The square was quite empty by now and he and the little group of men with him made their way across it without difficulty. They disappeared down one of the side streets. Owen's men moved unhurriedly after them.

They came up with Osman just where the street joined up with two others. The street was wider there and Owen's men found it easy to slip round the sheikh, separating him from his followers and surrounding him.

The sheikh looked up, startled.

"What is this?"

Owen stepped forward.

"Come with me," he said.

Then Osman understood.

He opened his mouth to shout. One of Owen's Sudanis put a hand over his mouth, preventing him. There was a little struggle and Osman half-dragged himself free.

"There will be blood!" he shouted.

"It will be yours," said Owen, and signalled to his men.

They closed round Osman and now he was silent. Muffled and tied, he was quickly shepherded away. For good measure Owen took several of his followers too. The others were left, startled and winded. One lay on the ground.

The passers-by at the end of the street had not even noticed.

Osman was taken to one of the cells beneath Owen's office in the Bab el-Khalkh. The building was the Police Headquarters and well away from the Old City. It was also big and strong. Just in case.

Owen, though, did not expect any difficulty. It would take some time for the news to get around. Osman's followers would have to get together; and Owen would see that they did not find that very easy. He had warned the Assistant Commissioner, McPhee, and together they would ensure that for the next two or three days the city was flooded with agents who would alert them at once to an assembly. By then perhaps Zoser would be caught. The crowd would have other things on its mind and Osman could be released.

It might even be possible to scare him into silence, although when he was brought to Owen's office in the early hours of the morning that did not seem very likely.

"There will be blood," he said again as he came through the door.

"There has been too much of that already," said Owen. "That is why you are here."

"There will be more," Osman promised.

"It is bad there is blood," said Owen, "either Moslem or Copt."

"Where there is a blood debt," said Osman, "there must be blood."

"There was no debt originally," said Owen. "There was just a foolish act."

Osman did not reply.

"A sacrilegious act," Owen pursued, "which you, as a holy man, ought to have done your best to prevent. Instead of encouraging it. And perhaps instigating it."

"I did not instigate it," said Osman haughtily.

"But you knew about it. He was one of your men."

Osman shrugged.

"He was his own man," he said, "in this."

"But you knew. And could have stopped."

"Why should I stop? It was only a Copt. Besides, have not the Copts—"

"Be quiet!" said Owen. "Such talk will not help you now. You allowed this thing to happen and so must bear some of the guilt."

"There is no guilt."

"You treated heavy things lightly," said Owen, "and that does not accord with the Book."

"You quote the Book at me?" Osman glared at him.

"I do. Where the Book itself is taken lightly the offender is not worthy of respect."

Osman was plainly taken aback. He had not expected things to go like this. Owen pursued his advantage.

"You have done wrong," he said, "and you must put things right."

"I?" said Osman. "I?"

"You."

"I have struck no blow."

"You have caused many to be struck. It must be stopped before someone is killed."

"Someone has been killed," said Osman. "A Moslem. By a Copt."

"That is for me," said Owen. "Not for you."

"There is a debt."

"Which I will see is paid."

"The Christians protect the Christians."

"And the Moslems too."

Osman looked at him.

"See that it is so," he said.

Owen did not reply. After a moment Osman said: "Why have you taken me?"

"While I am pursuing the offender I do not want blood on the streets."

"If you take me, there will be blood on the streets."

"It will be Moslem blood," said Owen, "and I would not have it so."

"What do you want?" asked Osman.

"I want you to hold your hand," said Owen, "for a time."

"Why should I do that?"

"I suggest you go to some holy place, preferably out of the city, and pray for forgiveness for the levity which started this business."

"What if I don't?"

"You will stay here. And if there is blood you will have to pray for forgiveness for that also."

Owen sent him back down to the cells to think about it. He did not expect Osman openly to agree but he thought it quite likely that the sheikh might indicate his willingness to accept Owen's proposition. He thought he saw in Osman, beneath the intransigence and fanaticism, a certain uneasiness as to his own role in the affair. "Lightness" was not an easy charge for a religious sheikh to bear, especially if he felt there was some justification for the charge; and in his heart of hearts, away from the public arena, Osman might well accept the need for some self-examination. Owen hoped so. He would probably try releasing Osman even if he gave no outward sign of acquiescence. That might, in fact, make it easier for him. And, of course, if he did stir up trouble he could always be put inside again. However, Owen did not want to do that if it could be avoided. It would be better if the sheikh went away quietly by himself.

The attacks on the Copts brought, as Owen had expected

they would, bitter representations from the Coptic community. Among the leaders who came to complain was Andrus.

"If you do not take action," he said, "we shall."

"You have said that to me before."

"And you took no action."

"I took action. But so did you."

Andrus looked shaken.

"What do you mean?"

"Did you not take action?" Owen pressed him.

"If we did," said Andrus, "who can blame us?"

"I blame you," said Owen. "Without your action there would not have been blood, Coptic blood, on the streets."

"I do not know what is this action you refer to."

"Don't you?" said Owen, looking him straight in the eye.

"No," said Andrus, returning the look.

Owen was not sure. The contradiction was direct and on the whole he believed Andrus to be an honest man. But he sensed an unease beneath the directness. Perhaps although Andrus had not been personally involved, he knew more than he pretended.

Andrus returned to the burden of his present complaints. They were the same as last time but with, probably, more justification. And whereas previously, under the shock of the immediate offense, he had been fiercely indignant, now there was a savage bitterness which was in a way more alarming.

He answered Andrus, as he had done the other Copts, with assurances and counsels of patience; and with a touch of iron.

"Do not be drawn into reprisals," he said as Andrus left, "or there will be trouble."

"Do you think we should just sit back and take it?" asked Andrus.

"There won't be any taking it. I'll see to that."

"I hope you will," said Andrus. "I hope you will."

Andrus's name, of course, appeared on the list that Nikos compiled. Owen was surprised to see how extensive the list was. The church seemed to be a microcosm of Coptic society, with representatives of all social layers. Perhaps because it was conveniently placed on the edge of the Old City closest to the modern, developed parts where the more well-to-do lived, there were surprisingly wealthy people in its congregation. The

Zosers rubbed shoulders with men with a hundred times their income. Another way in which the church was comprehensive was in the range of cultural levels among its members. Primitive fundamentalists like Zoser stood alongside sophisticated civil servants like Sesostris and Ramses. Sesostris Owen could understand; he was a fundamentalist too. But Ramses?

He asked Nikos about it.

"It's a very old church," Nikos said. "Lots of people prefer it."

Georgiades had another explanation.

"They all stick together," he said.

Owen could also understand that. A minority which believed itself to be persecuted might well stick together. It would look after its members, even erring ones like Zoser, especially if the grounds for the offence were ostensibly religious ones. Zoser appeared to be a man of few friends. Even so, in the diffuse community which centered on the church there might be those willing to shelter him.

It was worth checking. But he would have to go through them all one by one. That was a task to stretch even the Mamur Zapt's resources (especially with the Curbash Compensation Fund so depleted). There were so many of them. Where to start?

The obvious place to start was with the known agitators and trouble-makers. But when he asked Nikos to check the congregation against his other lists, Nikos said:

"That's no good. You won't find any. They're all respectable people."

"How do you know?" asked Georgiades.

"They're all Copts," said Nikos, but went to look in his files.

Georgiades sighed.

"Unfortunately, he's right," he said.

Copts were law-abiding. Their crime rate was far lower than that of any other community. Even with Owen's political definition, they came out below other national and ethnic groups. On the whole they saw the British as allies from the point of view of protection, as insurance against massacre, and as offering opportunities for advancement. They flocked into government service. Just as Jews, in other countries, were traditionally identified with financial services, so the Copts, in Egypt, were identified with the civil service. Their critics said there was no need for them to break the law; they made it. They were on the inside.

Like Nikos. A thought struck him. Nikos made the lists. He had drawn up the list of church members and he maintained the other lists too. Any name that was on the list was there because Nikos had put it there. Would it be surprising if some names were not on the lists?

A feeling of helplessness came over him. All investigations, no matter what the books said, depended on bureaucratic processes. Especially his kind of investigation. It was only partly the men he had out on the streets and in the bazaars, the special agents like Georgiades. All these would be useless without record-keeping and, more than that, record-keeping of the intelligent sort that Nikos provided. If you couldn't rely on that, how could you even start?

He came to a decision. He would start with Nikos's list. Until Nikos was found wanting Owen would continue to trust him.

But he might ask Georgiades to do a little independent checking.

Because of the heat all work stopped about lunch-time and the city came to a halt. The streets emptied, the shops shut, the donkey boys retreated into the shade, and government offices closed. Most people took a siesta. A few British officials, however, in whom northern habits died hard, preferred to go to one of the clubs and have a drink and lunch there. Owen was one of these.

He was unable to sleep during the day, and used the dead time to keep up with the newspapers and journals in the reading-room and to swim in the club pool while it was comparatively empty. Afterwards, about five, when the club started to fill up with people arriving for the daily hockey and cricket matches, played always, by personal decree of the Consul-General, in the cool of the evening, he returned to his office. The buildings were empty except for the occasional orderly and the Assistant Commissioner at the other end of the corridor, and sometimes Nikos working late, and he was able to get a lot of work done.

His friends, however, were familiar with his habits, so Mahmoud knew where to find him. Mahmoud was another one who didn't take a siesta and just at the moment, still simmering over the way Zoser had slipped through his fingers, he was driving his men hard. Even Mahmoud, however, could not get them to work in the afternoons and he too, like Owen, normally used the afternoons to catch up on desk work and reading. This afternoon, though, he had been unable to concentrate on the case he was preparing. His thoughts kept drifting back to Zoser. He kept analysing and re-analysing the probabilities. And then he had his idea.

"It's logical," he insisted to Owen when they met. "When he's not at home and he's not working, that's where he is. Why shouldn't he be there now?"

They were sitting outside at their usual table. The heat was beginning to go off the streets and the shadows were creeping out from the walls. It was still early, however, and they were the only ones at the tables.

"There are lots of places he might be," Owen objected. "He could be anywhere. He might have left the city altogether."

"No, he wouldn't have done that," said Mahmoud. "He's never been out of the city in his life. He would be frightened."

"OK, but there are lots of places in the city."

"He's a creature of habit," said Mahmoud, "and very rigid. He has a few basic routines which he sticks to. He keeps to the places he knows, the ones he feels confident in. That's why he could be there."

"Someone would be sure to come across him."

"They might not say if they did. Anyway, they might not come across him. It's always dark, there are lots of little odd corners and he probably knows it well."

"It's a possibility," Owen conceded.

"You see," said Mahmoud, "we've been assuming somebody is helping him and we've been going round all his contacts. It's easy because there are very few of them. Well, we've drawn a blank. We could have missed it, I know." Mahmoud thought of the way Zoser had escaped before and wavered slightly. "But I don't think we have," he said determinedly. "Not this time. We've not found anything because there isn't anyone else involved."

"There must have been someone else involved at some point. Someone put him up to it."

"Well, do we know that? Are we sure? Maybe he just heard about the Andrus business and took it into his head to avenge it. All by himself."

Mahmoud happily following a logical trail was a different Mahmoud from the one sensitive to charges of Egyptian incompetence. He had forgotten all about his previous difference with Owen and was now totally caught up with his argument.

"It's a possibility," said Owen. "I don't know I'd go any further."

The intuitive, Welsh side of Owen always responded to Mahmoud's Arab inspirationalism; the pragmatic English side damped it down.

"But do you think it's worth trying?"

"Well—yes."

"OK, then," said Mahmoud. "Will you help me?"

The Parquet, true to its French origins, was completely secular and made no distinctions among Cairo's many religions. Mahmoud, however, like most of the Parquet lawyers, was Moslem. Usually this didn't matter because the Parquet confined itself to criminal offences and there was no religious dimension involved. Occasionally, however, there was and then, Cairo being Cairo, the Parquet trod very carefully. Mahmoud clearly thought this was one of those times.

"You see," he said, "it's the church."

How would it look if a Moslem took his men into a Christian church on the pretext, as the Copts would see it, of conducting a search? Wouldn't it come perilously close to desecration? Almost as close, say, as putting a dog in a tomb?

But would it look any better if a Christian Mamur Zapt were to do it? In Cairo there was almost as much difference between Christian and Christian as there was between Christian and Moslem. And the Mamur Zapt wasn't even an Egyptian Christian.

There was another thing, too. So far he had been able to maintain a claim to even-handedness on the grounds that he treated both sides, Moslems and Copts, with equal severity. Wouldn't this be seen as tipping the balance?

Mahmoud was watching him anxiously.

If Zoser was hiding in the church and they caught him it would be worth it. But suppose he wasn't? They would have stirred up trouble for nothing. Just at a time when the Copts were especially sensitive.

Wouldn't it be better if Mahmoud did it? After all, it was the Parquet's business. Treat it as he would any ordinary issue and any ordinary criminal. If it had been a brothel or a gaming club Mahmoud wouldn't have hesitated. He would have sent his men in at once. Why couldn't he do that now?

But as soon as he posed the question, Owen knew the answer. Mahmoud was quite right. He couldn't do it. The Copts would object very strongly if Owen were to invade the church; but if Mahmoud did it they would riot.

"OK," he said. "I'll do it."

They moved fast.

This time they were taking no chances. Owen did not even go back to his office. He got Georgiades to bring his men to the Bab es Zuweyla and only then told Georgiades what he had in mind.

"OK," said Georgiades instantly.

He looked at Mahmoud.

"How many men have you got?"

"Ten."

"Get some more. Enough to put a ring round the church."

"I've got enough to watch the roads."

"Yes," said Georgiades, "but he won't use those."

Mahmoud found some more men and Georgiades showed him where to station them. Mahmoud was quite content to follow Georgiades on this. Good investigator though he was, he preferred to leave this side of the business to others. Georgiades would handle it better.

"If he comes running out," said Georgiades, "at least they'll see him now. Though whether they'll be able to do anything about it if they do see him . . ."

Georgiades had no high opinion of the police.

He gathered his own men into a little bunch and gave them careful instructions. He had used them before and they knew what to do. Intelligence was the thing in a case like this, not brawn. Intelligence—and speed. It would have to be done quickly. The more time they took, the more time there was for a crowd to gather. What Owen wanted was to be in and out fast.

The men rushed in and fanned out quickly. At least there wasn't a service going on. A few black-gowned priests looked up startled. For a moment or two they couldn't understand what was happening. Then one of them rushed off.

One of Georgiades's men intercepted him.

"Where are you going?" he asked.

"To fetch the Father," the priest snapped at him.

"You stay here," said the man.

The priests were shepherded into a little knot. They seemed completely bewildered. Bewildered first and then angry. It was not long before they began to complain.

As the angry voices rose higher and higher other black-gowned figures came in. Among them was an impressively-dressed figure whom Owen recognized to be the Father of the church. He went across to him.

"I am sorry, Father, that this should be so," he said. "We will not be long."

"Why are you here?"

"We are looking for an evil man."

"Here? In the church?"

"I am afraid so."

"But why here? What reason have you to look here?"

"One has told us."

It was easier to put it that way. To say that they were here only because of a hunch would not do at all.

"It is an outrage!" the Father said angrily.

"We will not be long."

Owen walked away. The Father joined the other priests. They crowded round him and began to talk excitedly.

"Have you thought what the Metropolitan will say?" said Georgiades in an aside as he hurried past.

The Metropolitan was the head of the Coptic Church in Egypt. He would not be pleased.

"And the Patriarch?" said Georgiades, the next time he went past.

The Patriarch. Owen had forgotten about him. The Patriarch was head of the whole Coptic Church, including the Abyssinian one, which was Coptic too. Abyssinian. There could be an international complaint. The Patriarch would use the country's ambassadors. They might go straight to the Foreign Office. The British Government would have to respond. And the British Government, churchgoers like Postlethwaite, would hardly be likely to take kindly to one of its servants invading a church. A Christian church, too.

Owen cursed himself for having been so foolhardy as to get involved in this affair. Why hadn't he stayed out of it? Got Mahmoud to go in? Even if Mahmoud had refused, would it have mattered so much? They could always have had the church watched and perhaps picked up Zoser when he came out. If he was there, that was. He might not even be there and the whole thing would have been for nothing and all he would have got out of it would have been kicks. This, he told himself, is a big mistake.

It began to look increasingly like it. Georgiades had split his force into two. The first group had taken up position in all the key intersections so that they could control anyone who attempted to pass. The second group had moved immediately into the *hekals,* the Coptic apses, of which there were many, screened off from the rest of the church by fine, heavily-pictured screens. Beyond there was the baptistery and beyond this a whole host of little rooms used by the priests. The men went methodically through these. They knew what to do. They were used to the job. They performed similar raids every week; not on churches, admittedly, but on printers' premises, warehouses, gambling dens, brothels and private houses. Garvin himself, before he became Commandant, had been responsible for training them. He had needed expert searchers for his battle against the drug traffic. There were none and he had had to train them. Once trained, they could be used for other things too.

Georgiades went past again. This time he didn't say anything. His brow was furrowed in concentration. The sweat ran down his face in streams.

His men were beginning to return from their searches. They came and stood in a little group, disciplined and obedient. Owen didn't need to ask. They had found nothing.

Georgiades, vexed, went off on a search of his own. His

second-in-command re-divided the men and sent them back for a second search of the places they had searched before. Owen had hoped to avoid this. It all took time.

He went to the door of the church and looked out. Already a little crowd had gathered. He saw Mahmoud, who caught his eye questioningly. Owen shook his head.

Back in the church the priests were shouting angrily at the men. The men, who were mostly Sudanis from the south, ignored them but looked uneasy.

Georgiades came back mopping his face. He stood in the centre of the church beneath the great dome and began to look carefully all round him.

The men, returned from the second time, stood waiting.

"Have you done the crypt?"

Georgiades nodded without speaking. His eyes were now on the roof.

The Father broke away from the knot of priests, shrugging off the efforts of the men to restrain him, and came across to Owen.

"I am not having this," he said.

Owen ignored him. He thought he could hear a growing murmur outside.

"You have no right!" the Father said hotly.

"The Mamur Zapt has the right," said Owen.

Strictly speaking, he was correct. The Mamur Zapt had right of entry to all premises in Cairo. However, it was a right which it was sometimes wise not to use.

"This is sacrilege!"

"My men have been very careful."

He turned away. The Father hesitated, looked for a moment as if he was going to come after him, then shrugged and rejoined the knot.

The door of the church opened. The murmur of the crowd became more distinct. Mahmoud came in.

"Soon," said Owen.

He would not be able to hold them for long.

Mahmoud went out. The door closed firmly behind him. He would hold the crowd as long as he could. Owen had no doubts on that score. But he was a Moslem and the crowd would be Copt. Owen himself would have to go out soon.

Georgiades made a sudden dart. There were no towers to the church, no staircases going upwards. But there would be access to the roof, if only for care and maintenance.

Georgiades had found out. It was a series of pegs in the wall going upwards. He began to climb. Two of his men followed him.

Georgiades was a bulky man, not good at this sort of thing. It would have been better to have let the men go first. He could see Georgiades stop to catch his breath. No doubt he was thinking the same thing. He went grimly on.

The pegs went up to the level of the bottom of the big dome. Now Owen looked, he could see a thin gallery running round it. It could be no more than a foot wide. In the darkness it was hard to see but it looked as if there wasn't even a railing.

"Light the lamps!" Owen said.

The men ran round the church seizing any lamp they could find. Some of them brought candles and torches. There were indignant shouts from the priests.

As the lamps were raised, the shadows chased back towards the top of the dome. In the less than half light Owen saw that Georgiades had come out onto the gallery.

There was a sudden shout. Below Georgiades his men leapt up the last few pegs. Georgiades began to go one way round the gallery, his men the other. Their shadows loomed grotesquely on the sides of the dome.

And with them another shadow, smaller, hunched, desperate.

The shadows converged.

And then, before they quite met, the smaller shadow seemed to detach itself from the wall and move out into space. It hung there for a moment. Then it fell.

CHAPTER 8

"Dead! In his own church!" said the Moslems with satisfaction. There was general agreement—among the Moslems—that justice had been done. It was accepted without question, even by the Copts, that Zoser had been the Zikr's killer and the Moslems were pleased that the matter had ended in such a satisfactory and clean-cut way. The British, it was agreed by all, on this occasion, were men of justice despite their many other faults, only they did have a habit of making tidy things untidy by over-insistence on bureaucratic process. Better that it should end like this, when justice was not only done but manifestly seen by all to be done.

Surprisingly, however, some Moslems, mostly at the upper end of the social scale, disagreed.

"It's this tax business," Paul explained, "this levy the Khedive is proposing. Word of it is beginning to get round and the Copts are already showing signs of growing restive. The Khedive is starting to realize that he might have trouble on his hands. So he doesn't want incidents like this."

"It's a mess," was the way Garvin put it later. "Administratively, I mean. It would have been better to have taken him prisoner. We could have delayed the trial until the tax business was settled. Then it wouldn't have mattered."

"Jane Postlethwaite wouldn't have been here to give evidence."

"You weren't planning to use her, surely?" said Garvin, rubbing his chin.

That was one good thing to come out of the affair. Jane Postlethwaite wouldn't have to give evidence. When the news was broken to her she suddenly went white. "Poor man," she said. "Poor, poor man." Zeinab took a more practical view. "It was a good job you didn't have to climb up that ladder," she said. "What ladder?" asked Owen. Zeinab was always imprecise about detail.

The reaction of the Copts was strangely muted. The Metropolitan, of course, complained—that was what Garvin was seeing Owen about. Various local delegations came to Owen to protest about the invasion of the church. Zoser was scarcely mentioned.

Andrus was a member of one of the delegations. On this occasion he said unusually little.

So far there was no word from the Patriarch, or from Abyssinia. Owen began to hope that they viewed the incident as too small to bother about. Perhaps it had not even been reported to them.

Mahmoud, busy as ever, had immediately switched to another case. It was clear that he regarded the matter as closed.

Owen was not so sure. Tit-for-tat exchanges between the communities of Cairo did not necessarily end just because a man had been killed. He was waiting to see if there were any further attacks.

As the days went by, however, and no further incident was reported, he began to relax. His words to Osman appeared to have had some effect. On the Copt side, too, all was quiet. One morning he went so far as to say to Nikos that he thought the affair was now over.

"Yes," said Nikos, "provided that it was the simple case."

"What do you mean?"

"The simple case," said Nikos, "is that the matter began and ended with the Zikr. He desecrated the tomb; he has paid for it."

"Well?"

"The other case is when it doesn't end there. Suppose Andrus were right? Suppose it were not the whole thing but part of a pattern? That gets more complex."

"Polo," said Paul.

"What?"

"Polo. It's a game you play on horses. There's a match tomorrow. Would you like to go and see it?"

"No!" said Owen.

"Pity. I've arranged for you to take Miss P."

"I don't want to watch polo. I've got better things to do."

"Hasn't everybody? However, that's not the point. I need

her out of the way tomorrow afternoon because things are reaching a juicy stage and I've got to work on her uncle."

"Couldn't you find somebody else?"

"I've picked you. Though not with the confidence I used to. However, with polo you ought to be all right. Just confine yourself to watching the game, that's all. If a horse has to be shot, or, I suppose, a rider—perhaps they do that sort of thing in polo; I expect they do since the Army has a hand in it—you don't have to go out of your way to ensure that she has a ringside seat. Nothing nasty this time, please."

"It will be very boring," Owen complained.

"I certainly hope so."

"Mightn't she find it boring too?"

"Oh, I don't know. There are the horses. Don't girls like horses?"

"I would have thought she'd have outgrown that."

"I would have thought so too, but last night I spent a whole dinner sitting between two girls who talked about nothing but horses. That's what gave me the idea."

"I think she may be different."

"So she may, and tomorrow's the chance for her to find that out. I've arranged for you to pick her up from her hotel at four o'clock."

The polo took place at the Khedivial Sports Club, or Gezira, as it was familiarly known, and the following afternoon found Owen walking dutifully about its spacious grounds with Jane Postlethwaite's hand resting lightly on his arm. He had been somewhat apprehensive about the encounter in view of the way their last meeting had ended, but fortunately she seemed to have put her irritation behind her. They stood beneath the trees for a while watching the game.

"Do you play polo yourself, Captain Owen?" she asked politely.

"A lot of people did in India," he said. Honesty compelled him to add: "I didn't. I couldn't afford the ponies."

Jane Postlethwaite turned her candid gaze upon him.

"They are very expensive, I presume?"

"Not in themselves. It's the things that go with them. Stabling, a syce—that's a sort of groom—that kind of thing. You couldn't really manage it on a subaltern's pay. Of course, most of the officers had private incomes."

The play moved over to the other side of the field and they stopped their conversation for a moment to follow it. Then a long hit sent ponies and riders thundering away.

"It seems wrong," said Jane Postlethwaite.

"What does?"

"To spend your money on this sort of thing."

"There are worse things to spend your money on."

"And better." She turned away. "Shall we walk through the grounds?"

The grounds were beautiful and well kept. There were marvellous flowerbeds, rose-gardens and herbaceous borders, well-established trees and shrubberies in full bloom. Yet the pride of the Gezira was its turf. Lush, green fields stretched in all directions. They were heavily watered each day in both the morning and the evening and kept their greenness in spite of the wear and the sun. All the pitches were lined with trees under which spectators could sit and which made splendid spots for picnics when no game was going on. There were several families under the trees now, with little children running around and babies crawling about in the grass. Jane Postlethwaite watched them with pleasure.

"I can see now," she said. "I can see how it might be possible to bring up a family here. I wondered how an English family could manage it. It's so hot. It would drain the energy out of you."

"You get used to it."

"Especially with children."

"Lots of men send their families home to England in the summer."

"I wouldn't like that," said Jane Postlethwaite with a decided shake of her head. "I wouldn't like that at all."

They made a wide circle through the grounds. By the time they came back to the club house the sun was already setting. Through the trees they could see the spectators returning from the polo. Because of the heat games never started before four and they had to finish soon after six because of the early Egyptian twilight. There was time for one innings only if you were playing cricket. All matches had to be two-day ones.

They approached the club house through a fine avenue of tall mimosas. Jane Postlethwaite dawdled.

"It's lovely," she said enthusiastically. "It's just like one of those avenues you sometimes see in Italy. Different trees, of course. But against the sky, especially when it's beginning to get dark . . . Have you ever visited Italy, Captain Owen?"

Owen hadn't. To him Italy was as alien and remote as—well, as England was. It was ten years since he had been in Europe. He had left England when he was nineteen. The landscape he knew was that of the East.

Jane Postlethwaite went happily up the steps of the club house and off to the ladies' room. Owen waited outside. At this time of day it was cooler outside than in the airless rooms of the club. He took a turn along a path between the great bougainvillaea bushes. A man came along the path towards him, obviously taking the air, as he was. He looked at Owen, stopped and stretched out his hand.

"Hello," he said. "Enjoying the polo?"

"The grounds more," said Owen.

It was Ramses, the civil servant from the Ministry of Finance whom he had talked to at the Consul-General's reception.

"Me too," said Ramses. "I bring my family out here for a picnic. The boys like watching but I can't say I greatly enjoy it myself."

They fell into step beside each other. Owen asked how John Postlethwaite was getting on in the ministry.

"All right. He's very thorough. He knows his stuff."

"I wish I did. Accounting has always been a closed book to me."

"I don't suppose it figures large in an officer's training."

"No. But when you move into administration you find you need it."

"All administration is ultimately money," said Ramses, who had a professional bias in the matter.

"Money. And people."

"The two go together."

"Especially in Cairo."

They both laughed.

"I'm having problems," said Owen.

"A soldier's pay doesn't go far," said Ramses neutrally.

"No, no. It's not that. I'm having problems with my viring."

"You don't have powers of virement, surely?"

"I've sort of had in the past."

Ramses grinned.

"But they've found out?"

"Yes, but I need to vire, if that's what you call it. I get my money through all sorts of old accounts. It might have been all right in the past but it doesn't work now."

"That's the problem with Egypt's finances as a whole," said Ramses. "And that, actually, is why Lord Cromer suspended all delegated powers of virement. Everyone was switching money from one account to another and usually into their own account as well."

"I'm not doing that. I'm just trying to make things work."

"You won't get them to agree to virement. What you'll have to do is to ask for your allocation to be increased."

"Garvin said I wouldn't get anywhere doing that. It's mixed up with the levy on Copts, apparently."

"The proposed levy. It's not been agreed yet. Yes, that's quite true. There's an across-the-board freeze on any increases in allocation until the levy business is settled. But there usually is at this time of year anyway. It's getting near the end of the financial year. You won't get any increase this year, but if you put in a good bid now you might get your allocation upped for next year."

"Well, thanks," said Owen. "It's now that I need it."

"That's what they all say. Including the Khedive."

They headed back towards the club house.

"It's not just the levy," said Ramses. "It's the general political situation. The levy's only a pretext."

"I thought the Copts didn't like it?"

"They don't. But that's not the only reason for introducing it."

"The Khedive needs money."

"He always does. No, it's not that either, though that also is true. No, the real point is to make it impossible for Patros Bey."

"Make what impossible?"

Ramses looked sideways at him.

"You haven't heard?" He hesitated. "I thought you would

have. Otherwise I wouldn't have spoken. Oh well, you'll soon know, or else you'll find out: the Consul-General is trying to get the Khedive to make Patros Prime Minister."

"A Copt?"

"It's all these people wanting increases in their allocations," said Ramses. "You need someone who is both competent at finance and honest. In Egypt the two don't usually go together. Especially in politicians."

"Just in Patros."

"He's come up through the ministry. The Consul-General knows he can trust him."

"He's one of the blokes that stops me viring?"

"That's right. Only he left the ministry some time ago to go into politics."

"Is he in favour of the levy or against it?"

"A good question, the answer to which the Coptic community would dearly like to know. The point is, however, that whether he's actually in favour of the levy or not, he can't accept the Prime Ministership while the issue is still on the agenda. He would lose all credibility with the Coptic community. So, if you don't want him to become Prime Minister you keep the issue on the agenda."

"Which the Khedive is doing."

"Which the Khedive is doing for different reasons. He just wants money to go to France. The politicians around him are encouraging him in his insistence on the levy because they want to stop Patros."

"And when is all this likely to be resolved?"

"It's coming up to the boil, I would say," said Ramses, "coming up to the boil."

"I went to a funeral yesterday," said Georgiades.

"I'm sorry. It—" Owen began.

Georgiades cut him off.

"On business."

"What business?"

"Zoser's. At least, it was his funeral. It was in the Mar Girgis. I thought I'd go and see who attended."

"And who did attend?"

"Pretty well the whole congregation. Top to bottom."

"Ramses?"

"And Sesostris."

"Andrus?"

"Certainly. And did a lot of talking afterwards."

"What did he say?"

"Couldn't get close enough. I didn't want to make myself too obvious. In view of my last visit."

"A lot of people there?"

"Yes."

"That worries me," said Owen, "a bit."

"It surprised me," said Georgiades. "I'd thought he was a loner."

"It looks as though, on this occasion at least, a lot of Copts identify with him."

"It might be just that he's one of their flock."

"Wife there?"

"A woman smelling of perfumes."

"Anyone talk to her?"

"I couldn't see what went on behind the screen. But she didn't come with anyone. And afterwards she left on her own."

"You don't know where she went?"

"As it happens," said Georgiades, "I do."

"You followed her?"

"No," said Georgiades. "I wanted to hear what the others were saying. I got someone else to follow her. A small boy. For a large reward."

"Not Ali? That boy in the cemetery."

"That little bugger," said Georgiades, "may be most places in Casiro but he's not everywhere. No, another urchin. Equally unscrupulous."

"Anyway, he followed her home?"

"That's right. She's moved, but not far. Still within a stone's throw of the Scentmakers' Bazaar."

"She could still be important."

"Yes. So I've set this boy up with a regular income. He's keeping an eye on her. Debit the Curbash Compensation Fund with a few more milliemes."

The Mamur Zapt winced.

Eventually Owen had to summon Yussuf.

"Yussuf," he said, "things can't go on like this. You'll have to sort things out between you and your wife."

"I have no wife," said Yussuf obstinately.

"Yes, I know all about that," said Owen, "but it won't do. We haven't had any decent coffee for days. Besides, it's depressing everybody."

That was true. Yussuf's unhappiness had spread a cloud over the whole orderly room. Normally it buzzed with cheerful conversation. The orderlies didn't do a lot of work but they did do a lot of talking, and their general cheerfulness had a lifting effect on the corridor as a whole. Owen would hear them as he sat at his desk; and if by some incredible chance all the bearers at once were sent out with messages and the orderly room fell empty he was at once conscious of a gap. Since Yussuf had fallen out with his wife, however, the sounds from the other end of the corridor had become more subdued. At first the other orderlies had merely seized upon it as an excuse for extra banter. Gradually, however, they had all been infected by Yussuf's low spirits and now the orderly room was an oasis of gloom.

Even McPhee, the Assistant Commandant, had noticed it and that morning he had come along to see Owen.

"We can't have this," he said. "It's depressing everybody. You'd better have a word with him. I'd do it myself but he's your bearer."

Although, strictly speaking, the bearers were not assigned to individuals and worked as a pool, carrying messages for anybody in the building, in practice they identified themselves with particular people. When Owen had first arrived in the building Yussuf had decided, unilaterally, to be his bearer and now it was a source of great pride to him that he was the one who carried the Mamur Zapt's messages. Owen did not in fact have many messages—he preferred to use the telephone—and Yussuf had time on his hands. It had seemed to him a natural extension of his duties, and somehow consistent with Islamic notions of hospitality, to assume responsibility for seeing that Owen was properly supplied with coffee. The same generous spirit had seen him extend his service to the rest of the corridor, and now the whole floor depended on it. When the service faltered, therefore, everyone along the corridor was afflicted; and Owen, as the person responsible in custom for Yussuf, was seen as the man to put it right.

What precisely he could do about it was not immediately clear since even the Mamur Zapt's writ did not normally extend to the domestic relationship between man and wife. The consensus along the corridor was that Yussuf's wife was all right really apart from her inability to produce any children and that this was the root of the trouble. The other bearers took the traditional view that the right thing to do was for Yussuf to get rid of her and find another one; but for reasons known only to himself Yussuf was reluctant to do this. A refinement was therefore suggested, namely that he should keep his first wife and merely add a second. Here too, though, there were difficulties. Yussuf couldn't afford it and his first wife wouldn't allow it. She had marched indignantly out when the proposal had been put to her and the matter had remained unresolved ever since.

"I have no wife," Yussuf repeated obstinately.

"Then it's time you did," said Owen. "Either take Fatima back or find yourself another woman."

Yussuf was silent.

"Fatima has faults," Owen pursued. "No woman is without faults. Nor no man either. You yourself, Yussuf, are not without blame. Fatima has been a good wife to you. For the sake of that, take her back."

Yussuf stared straight in front of him. He gave no sign of having heard.

"You have shown her you are a strong man, one who must be obeyed. If she didn't know that before, she will know it now. She has learned her lesson. Be just as well as strong, O Yussuf."

Owen had fallen into the familiar rhetorical style of the Arab. It was partly the language itself that suggested it. When he had first come to Egypt Garvin had insisted that he stay with an Arab family perfecting his Arabic. Owen had a facility for languages and had learned his lessons well. He spoke Arabic now without strain and from the inside, not needing to translate, thinking in the Arabic mode.

Yussuf stirred, responding, possibly, to the familiar patterns.

"She has done wrong," he said.

"Indeed she has," Owen agreed hastily. "But now she knows better."

"She should acknowledge her fault."

"And probably wishes to," said Owen, hoping that Yussuf's wife was not as formidable as his sister.

"She has not said so."

"Well," said Owen, "you can hardly expect her to."

"She will have to say so before I take her back."

"Do not be too hard," Owen counselled. "The wise man is merciful as well as just."

"If she acknowledges her fault," said Yussuf, with the air of one making a great concession, "then I will take her back."

Owen praised Yussuf's justness and mercifulness, wondering, however, whether such an acknowledgement could be secured.

"There will have to be someone to go between you," he said.

Yussuf was prepared to accept that.

"Though not Soraya," he added darkly.

"Who is Soraya?"

"My sister."

Owen thought that rather a pity as she had seemed very competent, quite capable of sorting out both Yussuf and his wife. However, this was a point Yussuf stuck on, so in the end it was agreed that they would ask Leila, the wife of the senior bearer. Privately Owen intended to make sure that she was given a very strong briefing beforehand. For the moment, however, it looked as if the matter was on its way to being resolved.

"Fatima will know," he said to Yussuf, "that she has a husband who is just as well as strong, merciful as well as just."

"She is a fortunate woman," Yussuf agreed.

"And you will take her back."

Yussuf hesitated.

"It—it may not be so imple, effendi."

"Why not?"

"Effendi—"

"Yes?"

"I have already pronounced the divorce," said Yussuf with a rush.

Under Islamic law it was possible to divorce by simple declaration. The husband merely had to say, in the presence of witnesses, "I divorce thee."

"Did anyone hear you?"

Yussuf hung his head.

"Yes, effendi."

It transpired that the whole street had been summoned to hear the declaration.

"That is a pity. However, you can revoke your word and take her back."

It was allowable under the law for a husband who changed his mind to receive his wife back without ceremony. Twice.

Yussuf's head dropped even lower.

"Effendi—"

"Yes?"

"It was the triple vow."

If the words were spoken once, or even twice, the woman could be taken back. When the words were spoken for the third time, however, the divorce was irrevocable. And that applied whether the words were spoken on separate occasions or all together. Thus if a particularly irate husband pronounced the words three times in the heat of the moment the divorce was permanent and could not be reversed.

"You said it three times?"

"Yes, effendi," said Yussuf unhappily.

"That's all right," said Zeinab, "it happens all the time."

"They say it three times?"

"Yes. And afterwards they're sorry. It's too late then, of course."

"He'll have to marry someone else."

Zeinab curled her legs up under her on the divan. "Why?"

"Because we can't go on like this. It's affecting everybody."

"I didn't mean that. I mean, why does he have to marry someone else? I would have thought it mightn't be too easy. You say he's got a bit of a reputation as a skinflint."

"I didn't say that. His sister did."

"Well, she should know. If it's true, he might find it difficult to get anyone to agree. Mothers are not going to let their daughters go to someone who's mean with money. A bit of beating is all right, you can put up with that, but if a man is tight with his money there's always trouble in the house. Besides, there's nothing in it for the family."

"I would have thought a family would have been only too glad to get an unmarried daughter off its hands."

"Not if they're going to come back again immediately because their husband is forever divorcing them."

"Yussuf's not like that."

"It's the money, you see," explained Zeinab, who tended to take a very practical view of these things. "A lot of families will say that as soon as he's got the dowry you'll get the girl back. And then you'll be worse off than when you started. You've still got the girl but you haven't got the money."

"Perhaps he'd be willing to take someone without a dowry. In the circumstances, I mean."

"Him? Yussuf? Not if what his sister says is true."

"If I leaned on him."

"That might help," Zeinab conceded.

"I could even pay the dowry."

"I'd watch that if I were you. Otherwise they'll all be doing it."

"There are lots of poor families."

"If you were prepared to pay the dowry—"

"It might be worth it."

"What I can't see, though," said Zeinab, "is why bother with all this? Wouldn't it be simpler just for him to marry Fatima again?"

"He can't. That's the whole point. He's used the triple vow."

"But that's no problem. I've told you. People are always doing it."

"But—"

"There's a way round."

"There is?"

"Yes. It's simple. What you've got to do is to get *her* to marry again. You go to a friend, or if you haven't got one there are people who specialize in it, and then you get them to marry her on condition that they divorce her immediately afterwards. Once that has happened you're free to marry her again."

"The triple vow doesn't apply?"

"Not anymore."

Seeing that Owen was having difficulties in getting used to

the idea, she took him by the hand and pulled him down beside her on the divan.

"It's all right," she said. "In fact, it's quite common. Men are always divorcing their wives and feeling sorry afterwards. So there's got to be some way round it."

"It happens all the time?"

"Sure," said Zeinab, snuggling down. "All the time."

And then the trouble started.

The first sign was slogans daubed on the wall of a *kuttub,* a religious school where small children went for their first instruction in the Koran. The slogans were in ill-formed, illiterate script and Owen at first put it down as the work of children; not the children who went to the *kuttub,* who were infants, but older youths.

"It's the youths," he said to the Moslems who complained. "I don't know what things are coming to. Children have no respect for their elders nowadays."

That at least they could agree with and went away shaking their heads, believing it to be merely another instance of the general moral decline which was overtaking the world. But when the slogans appeared on the wall of two mosques and camel dung was dropped on the entrance of one of them they were very angry and came back to Owen and said that these were godless young and should be put down. The connection with sectarianism was made gradually and only came after a succession of similar events. Women going to the mosque had their veils snatched off; a Moslem water-seller was set upon and beaten; Moslem stalls in the market were upset; and during the evening call to prayer a bell had been rung loudly.

Owen found it hard to take such incidents seriously.

"These things happen all the time," he said sceptically when Nikos came in to report them.

"And people don't notice them. But now they are. That's the difference."

Nikos also brought in some leaflets which his agents had confiscated.

"This is a difference too," he said. "This is the first time we've had ones like this for quite a while."

The leaflet accused the Moslems of kidnapping children and

using them for ritual purposes. Afterwards, it was alleged, the victims were placed in the children's brothels in which Cairo abounded. There was, of course, no point in trying to check the veracity of the allegations. The matter was mystic as much as factual, drawn from deep-lying sub-strata of racial prejudice and religious fear. Similar accusations were made at different times against all the churches. They surfaced at intervals, burned hot for a time and then slipped back underground, to be stored again in layers of social and religious memory.

If there were leaflets there was organization. And if there was organization there was money. And if there was organization and money, then there was design and planning. The incidents were not spontaneous. They were part of a pattern. He had hoped that the affair of the dog and the death of the Zikr were isolated instances, that with the death of those responsible the matter could end there.

It looked as if it was only beginning.

CHAPTER 9

The Moslem response was not long in coming. Fighting broke out in one of the markets, two people were stabbed and a third sprained his ankle when a stall of onions collapsed. The stab wounds were presented to Owen when he went down to inspect. Both victims were brought to him limp in the arms of their supporters and their condition appeared dire. However, closer inspection suggested that the volume of groans was in inverse proportion to the extent of the damage and Owen soon pushed them away. More important was the fact that one was a Copt and one a Moslem, which gave hope that, honour being satisfied on both sides, the exchanges might not be carried further. He lectured all sides sternly, posted a constable conspicuously, and went back to his office relieved that matters were no worse.

Over the next few days, however, there were a number of such incidents and some of them did not end so happily. There were other stabbings, some of them serious. Attacks on individuals became so frequent that there were notably fewer people on the streets after dark than was usual. Gangs of youths gathered outside shops. At first they contented themselves with shouting insults and throwing stones. Then one gang went further. It broke into a shop and wrecked it, terrifying the owner. After that, such attacks became the pattern and often, now, the attackers were not satisfied with merely terrifying the owners, they beat them up as well. One gang set fire to a shop after wrecking it and then that too became a feature of the attacks.

Similar incidents occurred all over the Old City and the manpower Owen could command was stretched to its limit. McPhee had all the ordinary police out in support and Garvin brought in extra police from the country districts around Cairo.

"We need more," said Owen. "It's still growing. That won't be enough."

"It's got to be enough," said Garvin. "There aren't any more."

"Can't you transfer some from Alexandria?"

"What happens if it spreads there?"

"It would be better to have city police. They're better at this sort of thing."

The country police were sufficiently confused simply by being in a big city, without adding in all the complex requirements of urban policing under riot conditions.

"Can't you grow your own?" asked Garvin. "Take more people onto your payroll?"

"Haven't the money," said Owen, remembering the Curbash Compensation Fund with bitterness. "I spoke to you about that."

"I suppose I could try again," said Garvin. "There might be some spare cash floating around since it's getting near the end of the year."

He rang back later.

"No chance," he said. "They're up to their eyeballs in balance sheets, especially with Postlethwaite looking over their shoulder, and won't even listen to me."

"They're all bloody Copts in the Ministry of Finance, that's the trouble," said Owen.

The pressure now, though, seemed to be coming from the

Moslem side. Crowds gathered outside the main mosques and there were huge demonstrations; spontaneous, according to the Moslems, organized according to Owen.

"Osman?" he asked Georgiades.

Georgiades nodded. He had been out on the streets all day and his face was running with sweat.

"Yes," he said. "Osman. Plus money."

The following evening there was a particularly ugly incident, although this time, against the tide, it appeared to be the Copts who were responsible.

It took place not at the Blue Mosque but further along the street in front of the great Mosque of el-Mouayad. Some Moslem students who had been visiting the mosque were set upon as they left by a much larger gang of Copts and in the fracas at least one of the students appeared to have been killed. Owen was unable to check every incident himself and sent one of his men over. The agent, a good one, reported that the affair wasn't quite as dramatic as first accounts had suggested and had been on a far smaller scale, but that students had definitely been involved and at least one of them appeared badly hurt. The involvement of students was something that Owen had been hoping to avoid. The students of el-Azhar, the great Moslem university of Cairo, were only too ready to take to the streets in defence of religion or, indeed, anything at all, and once they were participating it would be very difficult to keep the matter localized. His worst fears were realized when the next day word came from Georgiades that a monster procession was being formed which would march from the gates of el-Azhar through the Old City to converge on the Mar Girgis, where a demonstration was planned.

The only good thing about all this was that the procession was going to march through the Old City.

"It will be a shambles," Nikos confidently predicted.

And on the whole it was. The streets were thin and crowded anyway. When hundreds of students tried to proceed along them they very speedily became totally blocked. The organizers of the march had foolishly neglected to warn the shopkeepers in advance, with the result that shops were still open and their goods, as was the custom with Cairo shops, spread across the pavement. Agitated shopkeepers rushed out into the street when they saw the marchers approaching and tried to rescue their wares. The marchers, who were initially good-humoured, slowed down in an effort to help. Those behind ran into those in front, some tried to crowd past, and in a very short time the result was, as Nikos had forecast, a shambles. One bewildered donkey was enough to block off a street—and that was without any help from Owen.

The marchers became impatient with the slowness of their progress and spread into neighbouring streets. These filled up and blocked too and the whole Old City was brought to a standstill. Confused marchers mingled with bewildered shoppers, excited but ill-informed spectators tried to sort things out and soon everything was in total chaos.

It was hours before the first students managed to permeate the streets and come to within a hundred yards of the Mar Girgis.

Where Owen was waiting. McPhee had put carts across all the streets leading to the church, barricading them completely. In front of each barricade a row of hefty constables was drawn up with truncheons in their hands. Behind the carts were other men. Owen took care to let the demonstrators see that these were armed.

The demonstrators came to a halt. Because they had arrived independently and in twos and threes they had outstripped their organizers and were at a loss what to do. As their numbers grew they formed a wedge between the barricades and the main body of the procession, which was forced to stop short some way away from the barricades.

Owen could see the head of the procession from where he stood. It appeared to be carrying something.

It was some time before the organizers were able to sort things out. Eventually, however, they managed to open a channel in the wedge and bring the leaders through to the barricades. Among them was Osman.

Owen could see now what they were carrying. It was a stretcher. On it was a pale-faced corpse with an arm flipping over the edge of the stretcher. The corpse was that of a young man. Presumably the student had died.

As it approached, the cries of the students rose to a frenzy. Everywhere now was a sea of raised fists and shouting faces.

Banners tossed and lurched among the faces. The first stone hit the carts.

Osman Rahman pushed his way forward.

"Why have you done this?" he said, pointing to the carts.

"To stop you from going any further," said Owen. "Tell your people to go home."

"They have a right," Osman protested angrily.

"Tell them to exercise their rights peacefully."

Osman turned round and began to harangue the crowd. He was, of course, telling them no such thing. He was using the opportunity to denounce the British as well as the Copts, bracketing them together as Christians combining against true believers. The voice rose on a wave of passion. Owen could not tell whether this actually was the demonstration, conveniently moved in view of the circumstances, or whether Osman meant to whip thing up to the point when the crowd would storm the barricade. The rhetoric was violent enough. On the other hand Osman was a practised orator and knew what he was doing. The crowd had settled to listen to him. No more stones were being thrown.

The stretcher was being passed over the heads of the crowd. Once or twice as a hand grabbed and missed it lurched and threatened to tilt the corpse onto the crowd. Somehow it always righted itself and reached the front, where new hands seized it and raised it high so that everyone could see it. There was Osman, raised on the knees of his supporters, and the corpse limp on the stretcher beside him.

From time to time Osman turned and gesticulated at the stretcher and every time he did so a cry of anger rose from the crowd. The constables twitched apprehensively.

McPhee slid along in front of them and stood beside Owen.

"Do we wait?" he said. "Or do we hit them before they come to the boil?"

Although McPhee, as Assistant Commandant, was nominally ranked higher than Owen, in operations of this sort the Mamur Zapt, responsible for order in the city, was in control.

Owen was undecided. It was usually best to break up a demonstration in the early stages. It might already be too late. On the other hand it could still all end peacefully.

Out of the corner of his eye he saw the stretcher give a great jump. One of the arms holding it was getting tired.

Something about the corpse attracted his attention.

The stretcher jerked again.

The corpse seemed to brace itself against the tilt but that could not be, unless—

Owen watched it carefully and waited for the arm to tire again. When the jerk came he was ready for it.

"Have you a cigarette?" he asked McPhee.

McPhee was surprised.

"Thought you didn't smoke," he said.

However, he fumbled in his pocket and produced his usual cheroots.

Owen had seen it done during his time in Alexandria, where hysterical prostitutes were quickly restored to life and reason by an experienced old Austrian police officer of the Labban red-light quarter.

He lit the cheroot and, concealing it in his curved palm, edged towards the stretcher. The corpse's hand hung stiffly over the side.

Owen pressed the glowing end of the cheroot on to the dead man's hand. If things were as they seemed it wouldn't matter.

The "corpse" shot upright with a yell. As it did so the deathlike covering of flour fell from its face.

There was a moment or two of stunned silence. And then the crowd began to laugh.

The next morning the episode was the talk of all the bazaars in Cairo; and the bazaars enjoyed it greatly. From the bazaars the tale passed via servants into households and thence to the clubs, not so dissimilar from bazaars in their capacity to retail and embellish a story. Word came that the Sirdar liked it and Garvin was obliged to pass on to Owen a note of approval from the Consul-General.

"At least no one was killed," said Garvin sourly.

More to the point, the affair earned Owen a few days' breathing space. Not everyone in the Old City was an admirer of Sheikh Osman and there were quite a few Moslems as well as Copts who rejoiced in his discomfiture. For a few days Osman could not bring himself to show his face in public and there was a noticeable lull in hostilities.

"It won't last," said Georgiades. "Some brainless Copt is sure to attack a Moslem."

"Or vice versa," said Nikos.

Meanwhile Yussuf's affairs were progressing. The go-between had produced some degree of accord. Yussuf's wife, Fatima, was flattered by Owen's interest in the state of her marital relationship and after some hard bargaining agreed to return to Yussuf. The only problems now were technical. Here, too, progress was made. A man was found, a friend of one of the bearers, named Suleiman, who agreed—for a consideration—to become the temporary bridegroom. Yussuf applied to Owen, who, after swearing aloud to Allah that never again, under absolutely any circumstances, etc., etc., found the necessary money. And the very next day Yussuf, supported, as was proper, by every bearer in the place, went forth to tie and untie and retie the marital knots.

An hour or so later Owen was working peacefully in his office when the door slammed at the end of the building and feet came running along the corridor.

A bearer burst into the room.

"Effendi! Oh, effendi! Something terrible has happened!"

"Has Suleiman pulled out?"

"Oh no, effendi."

"The marriage went ahead?"

"Yes, effendi. But afterwards—"

"Yes?"

"He wouldn't divorce her."

"Not divorce her?"

"No, effendi. He said he had changed his mind. He said that Fatima's beauty was like the moon and the stars—"

"Yes, yes. He refused to use the vow?"

"That's right, effendi. We pleaded with them. We said it was wrong. But Suleiman said that Fatima's beauty—"

"OK, OK. The upshot is they're still married?"

"Yes, effendi. Suleiman said—"

"We've had that."

The bearer looked injured.

"—that it wouldn't have counted anyway because he would not have been able to use the words with a true heart."

"Of course it would have counted."

"That's what we said, effendi. But he wouldn't listen to us."

"Bloody hell!" said Owen.

"They went back to Suleiman's house," said the bearer, gratified, "and barred themselves in an upper room. We heard them laughing, effendi. And then they made the noises."

Yussuf was in a state of deep shock. Later in the afternoon Owen went along to the bearer's room. He found Yussuf squatting on the floor with his back against one of the walls staring dazedly into space. He did not even look up.

Both Georgiades and Nikos made use of the lull.

"I've found out something," said Georgiades, coming into the office the morning after the crash of Yussuf's hopes.

"What?"

"Where Osman gets his money from."

Owen laid his pencil down.

"The Goldsmiths' Bazaar. He's taken to going there regularly."

"To borrow?"

"I wouldn't have thought so. To be given."

"Who's giving it him?"

"A Jew."

"A Jew? Odd, that."

"He's obviously just an intermediary."

"He gets the money from someone else and passes it on to Osman?"

"That's right. That's my guess, anyway."

"Have you talked to the Jew?"

"Not yet."

"Will he talk?"

"He might."

"It would be interesting to know who he gets it from."

"Want me to ask?"

"Might be better to wait. Have you got a man on him?"

"Yes."

"Leave it like that for a day or two."

Nikos had been busy too, and he summoned them to show them the result of his labours.

On the wall in his room was a large map of Cairo. Pinned to it were a lot of little paper flags. Each flag stood for an "incident," green for Moslem-inspired ones, red for those initiated by Copts.

"Notice anything?"

The geographical pattern was clear. Four-fifths of the flags were within half a mile of the Bab es Zuweyla, the Old Gate, near which was both the Blue Mosque of the dervishes and the old church of the Copts, the Mar Girgis. Nikos had marked the church in white, the mosque in blue.

"Osman territory," said Owen.

"And Andrus territory?" asked Georgiades.

Owen looked at Nikos.

"Mar Girgis territory, at any rate," said Nikos. "A church is the centre of any Coptic network, and all the incidents fall in the territory that the Mar Girgis covers."

"Someone at the church, then. Not the priests—"

Uncomfortable memories of what had happened on his last visit to the Mar Girgis flooded into Owen's mind.

"No, no, no. They don't go in for this sort of thing. Someone else. Someone in the congregation. They're in the congregation so they naturally think of using the network. It's the sort of thing a Copt would think of, the sort of way they think."

"Zoser was in the congregation," said Owen.

"Yes," said Nikos, "that's one of the things I had in mind."

"And Andrus."

"That too."

"The Zikr," said Georgiades, "was in Osman's congregation. In a manner of speaking."

"Is that it, then?" asked Owen. "Is that what's happening? Andrus and Osman are slugging it out?"

CHAPTER 10

"It's hotting up again," said Garvin.

"Yes," said Owen, "I know."

"Pity. I was hoping you'd got it under control."

"It was just a lull."

"It didn't take long for him to bounce back."

"Someone's feeding him money."

"Any idea who?"

"Not yet. We think we know how but we don't know who."

"Only a question of time, then. The trouble is," said Garvin, "that time is exactly what you haven't got."

"It's still two weeks to the Moulid."

Garvin brushed it away.

"Not that. The Consul-General's been on to me. He would like things to quieten down."

"Well . . ."

"Yes, I know," said Garvin. "Wouldn't we all? Only I gather he's got a special reason for wanting it just now."

"Are we allowed to know what it is?"

Owen waited while Garvin thought it over.

"No," said Garvin finally. "I don't think so. Political. At the top."

"These things have a way of working down."

"And then a way of leaking out."

"The effect, I meant. Not the information."

"The information won't help you. Still," said Garvin, relenting, "I could tell you something, I suppose."

He liked to remind Owen that, out on a privileged limb though the Mamur Zapt might be, he, Garvin, had access to levels that Owen could only aspire to.

"It's to do with the succession," Garvin said. "The Consul-General wants the Khedive to reshuffle his Cabinet. And he has a particular person he would like to see become Prime Minister."

"Patros?"

Garvin looked at him in surprise.

"You know?"

"I had an inkling."

"Well," said Garvin, recovering, "I suppose it's the sort of thing you ought to have an inkling of. Though it's meant to be secret. Well, then, you'll know why just at the moment the Consul-General doesn't want trouble between Moslems and Copts."

"There's always trouble between Moslems and Copts. It's a fact of life."

"Yes, I know. But at some times it's apparent and at other times it's not. I want this one to be one of the times when it's not."

"You can't just damp these things down."

"Can't you? I thought you just had."

"I was lucky. And it earned us a lull, that was all."

"Earn us another one, then," said Garvin, "only a bit longer this time."

Owen wanted to say it couldn't be done. Wisely, he didn't.

"OK?"

"How much longer?"

"It's hard to say. A month?"

"The Moulid's in two weeks' time."

"Ah yes," said Garvin. "I was forgetting." He frowned and fidgeted with his pencil. "I'll talk to the CG," he said. "Mind you, I'm not promising anything. There's a complete log-jam at the moment."

"The levy business?"

"Yes. The Khedive won't agree to anything until he's got that."

"Why is he insisting on that?"

"Because he wants the money."

"Yes, but why does it have to be raised by means of a levy?"

"Because otherwise it would have to be financed through a general increase in taxation. That would increase the Khedive's unpopularity, and he's unpopular enough already. Whereas if he raised it through a levy on Copts that would be wildly popular with everyone else. His ministers are telling him it's a masterstroke. They're Moslem, of course."

"So he's not going to give way?"

"No. And nor is Patros."

"So it could take some time?"

"That's right."

"And the Moulid is in a fortnight's time."

"I'll do my best."

"If the Khedive got his money in some other way," said Owen, as he turned to go, "would that help?"

"If I were you," said Garvin, "I'd stick to the Curbash Compensation Fund."

Mahmoud rang, puzzled.

"What's going on?" he said. "They've put me back on the Zikr case."

"I'm still on it," said Owen.

"I thought that one had been settled. Didn't Zoser—?"

"Yes."

"Then why—?"

"It might be part of a bigger picture."

"Connected with what's going on at the moment?"

"Possibly."

"Have you found a connection?"

"No."

"Then I don't suppose I shall. Still, if that's what they want, I'll go through it all over again.

Afterwards Owen wondered why Mahmoud was back on the case. Could it be that someone had an interest in keeping it alive? Probably not in the Parquet itself. Higher up, almost certainly. The Minister? Anxious that no opportunity for keeping relations between Copts and Moslems on the boil should be lost?

"Don't you have a guilty feeling?" asked Paul.

"No," said Owen. "What should I have a guilty feeling about?"

"Jane Postlethwaite. You've been neglecting her."

"No, I haven't. I'm always seeing her."

"You haven't seen her this week."

"I've had one or two things on this week. Like the whole of Cairo up in arms."

"Keep these things in perspective. Remember what I told you. Jane Postlethwaite is important."

"Her uncle is important, I see that. Our jobs at stake, etc."

"More than that. Your whole life, for instance. Aren't you missing a chance?"

"What chance am I missing?"

"Jane Postlethwaite."

"Look, she's a nice girl, but—"

"She's a nice girl and. And her parents are dead, and her uncle is rich and influential, and for some strange reason he is quite attached to you, and Jane Postlethwaite is quite attached herself, and it's time you got maried—"

"Oh, come on."

"It is. You're quite old—"

"Oh really."

"You are."

"I'm just over thirty."

"You see? That's quite aged. Especially in this climate. Maturity becomes senility very quickly here. It's the heat and the sex and the drink. I've noticed it in a lot of my friends. Besides—"

"For goodness' sake!"

"—you need to get married if you're going to go any higher. At the top a single man is suspect. You wonder what he does with his time. Is he quite sound? And who will look after the entertaining?"

"Some brainless aide-de-camp. There are lots of those around."

"Do not try to deflect me. We were talking about your career, in which I am taking a fatherly interest. Besides, I want you to take Jane Postlethwaite to the opera tomorrow night."

"I can't. I'm taking Zeinab."

"Take them both. Jane Postlethwaite hasn't met many Egyptian women. She certainly hasn't met anyone like Zeinab."

"Can't you get someone else?"

"No. I've tried. None of the army officers will do because they're all tone deaf. Besides, opera isn't British."

"How do you know Jane Postlethwaite will like it?"

"She sings, doesn't she? I thought all Nonconformists did. You hear them on a Sunday morning."

"Yes, but that's different. It's a different sort of singing."

"There you are! A Welshman knows that sort of thing by instinct. Just the chap. Pick her up from the hotel at nine tomorrow."

Jane Postlethwaite was not sure about opera. She had not, she confided in Owen, actually been to one before and the glamour and glitter plainly made her uneasy. Since the plot had the usual operatic complication he had advised her to read the programme notes beforehand, and she perused them with a certain grim incredulity. When the audience broke into applause on first beholding the characteristically extravagant set she at first appeared dumbfounded and then sat back in her seat rather stiffly. However, as the evening progressed she seemed to relax and even to be enjoying the music.

Zeinab, on the other hand, entered into the opera totally. Dramatic herself, she enjoyed drama in art; and the music swept in over emotional defences that were already down. Owen could hardly bear to look at her, so much was she at the mercy of the music, plunging with it into pits of despair, rising with it to heights of exaltation that were almost unbearable. By the time they reached the interval she was already emotionally shattered.

Intervals were always protracted in Cairo. The whole performance, which started late anyway because of the heat, sometimes went on till four in the morning. So there was plenty of time to leave the box and promenade around.

Owen saw several people he knew. Hadrill, for instance, the Adviser to the Ministry of Justice. Should he ask him what was going on at the top of the ministry and why they were resurrecting the Zoser case? But Hadrill was carrying a huge score and looked as if he took opera seriously. Then there was an aide-de-camp, slightly bored, piloting a bemused, middle-aged group to a table which had already been set out with refreshments. Important visitors, clearly. Owen started taking Jane and Zeinab across to join them but on the way they ran into a group of journalists whom Zeinab knew and got into conversation with them. They were all a-bubble with the opera and the state of the arts in Cairo generally and Jane Postlethwaite was a bit out of it. Fortunately he saw a nice couple from the Ministry of Education and was able to guide her over to them. They were talking to a Coptic family, parents and two children.

"Hello," said Ramses, turning round, "how's the Curbash Compensation Fund?"

"What?" said the man from the Ministry of Education, whose name was Lampeter.

"Captain Owen is deep in the toils of the accountants just at the moment."

"Same here," said Lampeter. "It's the end of the year."

"I'm deep in the toil of accounts too," said Molly Lampeter. "It's the end of the month. Do you like opera?" she asked Jane Postlethwaite.

"I'm new to it."

"I was new to it when I came out here. Now I like it quite a lot."

Back among the journalists Zeinab caught Owen's eye and pulled a face.

"Is your friend Sesostris here?"

"Sesostris isn't here," said Ramses, "and he's not my friend."

"Where does he stand in the War of the Succession?"

"Out on a limb in my view. He's completely opposed to any Coptic participation in the Government."

"Even at the personal level?"

"You mean Patros? Yes. Especially."

"Is that going to happen soon?"

"Is it going to happen? A lot of people are keen to stop it. Including Sesostris."

"The Khedive will have to make up his mind soon."

"Or have his mind made up for him."

"Is that likely to happen?"

Ramses smiled and turned away.

They resumed their seats and Owen slipped away into a tide of music and colour.

When the opera ended Zeinab sat on, emotionally drained. Owen waited as usual for her to recover, talking quietly meanwhile with Jane Postlethwaite, who stole a glance at her from time to time, sympathetic and concerned but also slightly at a loss.

Zeinab caught one of her glances.

"I'm sorry," she said, smiling. She was beginning to recover. "It's always like this."

"Are you all right?"

"Oh yes. It's just the music."

"You feel it very deeply."

"Yes. Don't you?"

Jane Postlethwaite considered.

"No," she said. "I love the music, of course, the arias especially. But I don't feel—I don't get bowled over by it, in the way you do."

"The terribleness of it," said Zeinab, astonished and slightly losing her English, "you don't feel?"

Jane Postlethwaite looked uncomfortable.

"No," she said. "Very English of me, I'm afraid."

Zeinab laughed.

"And very Arab of me, too, I expect," she said.

"Not just Arab," said Jane Postlethwaite. "Italians are like it too. Especially about opera."

"You have been to Italy? And seen the opera?"

"I have been to Italy. I went last year with my uncle. But I'm afraid I did not go to the opera."

"No?" Zeinab was astounded.

"Perhaps I should have gone. But really I was there to look at the pictures."

"There are no pictures in Cairo," said Zeinab.

"But there are beautiful buildings. Some of the mosques are so lovely."

"I have never been to Italy," said Zeinab.

"It's not unlike here in some ways. There was a beautiful avenue of mimosas I saw at the Gezira when we were walking round. It reminded me so much of Italy, as I told Captain Owen."

"Ah."

Zeinab had not heard about this.

"I took Miss Postlethwaite to see the polo," he explained.

"Indeed?" said Zeinab distantly. She removed her hand from Owen's arm, where she had placed it.

"Against the deep blue of the sky just when it was getting dark," said Jane Postlethwaite enthusiastically. "So like Italy. And so romantic."

"Romantic," said Zeinab, as if she was taking the word down to be used in evidence.

"The desert makes a difference of course," said Owen.

"For better or worse?" inquired Zeinab.

"It's the contrast," said Jane Postlethwaite. "It shows up the differences."

"You think so?" Zeinab was inclined to take this personally.

Jane Postlethwaite caught the tone and stopped, startled. Zeinab rose to her feet and swept out of the box.

At the hotel Jane Postlethwaite made it worse by inviting them to tea on the following afternoon.

"I know you're busy in the morning," she said to Owen.

"Her or me," said Zeinab.

"What?"

"Either her or me. Not both."

"Don't be silly."

"I don't care if you have an affair with her but—"

"I'm not having an affair with her."

"Then how does she know you're busy in the morning?"

"Everyone knows I'm busy in the morning. I work."

"You took her to the polo."

"I had to take her to the polo. Paul made me."

"You shouldn't have taken her like that."

"Like what? Christ, there's no other way of taking her."

"Without telling me."

"Look. I don't tell you everything I do."

"No," said Zeinab, "you don't."

"I tell you the things I think will interest you."

"If you go out with another woman that interests me."

"I'm not going out with another woman. Not like that."

"Not like what?"

"Not like you're supposing."

"What am I supposing?"

"For Christ's sake!"

Zeinab started on another tack.

"She is cunning, that girl."

"Nonsense."

"Why is she here? Tell me that."

"She is here to accompany her uncle. And besides, Egypt is an interesting place to visit."

"She is here to get a husband. Like the others."

Zeinab had no high opinion of the scores of English girls who flocked over to Egypt during the Cairo season and flirted with the deprived and well-connected young army officers.

"She is not like them," said Owen.

"Oh? And how is she not?"

"You can tell it straightaway."

"Well, tell it then."

Owen found this unexpectedly difficult.

"She is more modest," he said lamely, "more shy and retiring."

"More cunning," said Zeinab.

"She is a Nonconformist."

Zeinab was stopped in her tracks.

"What is this? This 'Nonconformist'?" Under the strain of the occasion Zeinab's accent was becoming more and more French. "She is Socialiste? Nationaliste? Her? I do not believe you."

"It is religious." It suddenly struck him that this was not perhaps the best time to go into the history of the Established Church in England. "A sort of sect."

"Ah. Like the Copts."

"No," said Owen, "not like the Copts."

"If I were you," said Zeinab, "I would have nothing to do with Copts. Or Nonconformists."

Things were indeed hotting up again; and they seemed to Owen to be hotting up chiefly on the Moslem side. Osman had recovered from his put-down and seemed bent on recovering the ground he had lost. There were incidents everywhere, in the bazaars, in the street markets, outside the churches, in the squares. The incidents were beginning to involve more people, too. That took organization; and that took money.

"He's got more money than I have," complained Owen after four largeish simultaneous demonstrations had stretched his resources to the utmost. "Where the hell does he get it from?"

"He must have powerful friends," said Georgiades, who had just limped in off the streets; not injured but footsore. He wiped the sweat off his face with his sleeve and looked around hopefully. Nikos took pity on him and went out into the corridor and called for Yussuf. After a very long time Yussuf appeared. Since the débâcle of the wedding/divorce he had become very morose, hardly responding to outside stimuli at all, sunk in his pain and brooding on his wrongs.

"Coffee at once!" said Nikos sharply. He was not one to make allowances.

Yussuf shuffled off and Georgiades waved a grateful hand.

"I thought you had powerful friends too," he said to Owen. "Where are they?"

"They've got problems," said Owen, "and I'm beginning to wonder whether their problems and our problems are connected."

He told Nikos and Georgiades as much as he could about the current political log-jam, leaving out the Patros bit.

"You think there's someone on the Moslem side who's got an interest in keeping things on the boil?" asked Georgiades.

Owen nodded.

"There's a lot of money washing around," said Nikos. "Do you think it could be the Porte?"

Egypt was still in principle a province of the Ottoman Empire; and while the Khedive's allegiance to the Sultan of the Sublime Porte was in practice nominal, the Turks took a keen interest in Egyptian affairs.

"No real sign of that so far. I think it's internal."

"Well, one thing's for sure," said Georgiades. "It's not the Khedive. He hasn't any money."

"Not many of them have, at least not on the Moslem side. That's why I think it could be a group of them acting together. Ministers, perhaps, who don't like the way things are going."

"Any evidence of that?"

"Well," said Owen, "I don't know if this is evidence, but . . ."

He told them about Mahmoud being put back on the case.

"It must be someone high up," said Nikos. "The case has been formally closed."

"The Minister?"

"Could be. He's new and ambitious."

"Any money of his own?"

"Not of his own. He might be able to lay his hands on some."

"Especially if he was doing it with a few friends."

"It's a bit out of our range, isn't it?" asked Georgiades. "I mean, if it's a minister?"

"The Consul-General's in this particular political game too," said Owen, "and I think he would be interested."

"How do we find out?"

"The only line we've got is through Mordecai," said Nikos.

"The Jew?"

Nikos nodded.

"In any case it would be interesting to find out where the money's coming from," said Owen.

"Find out," said Georgiades, "and stop it. Because if you don't, there could be big trouble. A few more demonstrations like those last night and the whole place could get going."

"I think," said Owen, "it's time I had a word with Mordecai."

The workers in gold spilled out of the Goldsmiths' Bazaar and into the surrounding streets and alleyways. As you approached the bazaar you passed their showcases, full of the flimsy and barbaric workmanship which the native Egyptians admired. There were bracelets and anklets of great weight and solidity made of the purest gold. These were investments and the form in which less-educated Egyptians stored their savings. There were, too, rings and earrings and charms, charms especially, which the Egyptians loved.

Mordecai's stall was on the very edge of the bazaar. You stepped down into it out of the street. It was lit by candles, and in the soft light the gold in the showcases round the walls shone three-dimensionally, given depth by the shadows. Mordecai himself was so much part of the shadows that at first when you stepped into the shop you did not see him. Then a little move, a little cough, made you aware of his presence.

He led Owen into a recess behind a recess. There was hardly room for the two of them, let alone for Georgiades, who followed them in but had to remain stuck in the doorway. In the confined space Owen was powerfully aware of the heavy smell of body oil which, like many Egyptians, Mordecai used in abundance. As the moments went by he became aware of another smell, that of sweat. For Mordecai was sweating profusely. He was scared.

"You know who I am?"

Mordecai moistened his lips.

"Yes, effendi. The Mamur Zapt."

"Very well, then. You know what I can do. You need not fear, however. You are only a little player in a game in which there are big players. I am not interested in little players. When you have told me what you know you can go. Provided that you tell me truly."

"Effendi . . ." Mordecai hesitated.

"Yes?"

"What of the big players? What will they do to me?"

"I am here. They are not."

The beads of perspiration streamed down Mordecai's face.

"They will kill me."

Owen said nothing. Just waited.

The smell of sweat was overwhelming.

"I will tell you. But . . ."

"Afterwards?"

Mordecai nodded.

"Do you have friends in another town? Say, Alexandria?"

"Yes, effendi."

"I will have you taken to them."

Mordecai looked relieved.

"Afterwards. Provided I am satisfied."

"Yes, effendi."

"Very well, then. Now tell me: there is a sheikh who comes to you and you give him money?"

"Yes, effendi."

"The dervish sheikh?"

"Yes, effendi."

"How much money have you given him in the last three weeks?"

"One hundred and thirty pounds. Egyptian."

Owen could sense Georgiades's astonishment. One hundred and thirty pounds was a lot of money in a country where an average wage was three pounds a month.

"That is a lot of money. It is not yours."

"No, effendi."

"Whose is it, then?"

"Effendi, I—I do not know."

"Come, it is not not here one moment and suddenly here the next. Where does it come from?"

"One brings it."

"That is better. And who is that one?"

"Effendi, I do not know him. I do not know the name, or from where he comes, or from whom he comes. All I know is that every Friday at a set hour he comes and puts the money into my hands. He never speaks. He merely takes the receipt, then goes."

"Does he give you no instructions?"

"Never."

"Then how do you know you are to give it to the Sheikh Osman?"

"It was told me before."

"When was this?"

"A month ago. A man came and said to me, one will come with money and you will do thus and thus."

"Who was the man?"

"He was but a bearer."

"But not the same as the bearer who brings the money?"

"Not the same, effendi. The first one was but a servant. The one who brings the money, well"—Mordecai hesitated—"I do not know what he is but he is not a servant."

"The one who brings the money: can you tell me something else about him?"

"Only," said Mordecai, "that he is a Copt."

"A Copt?"

"Yes, effendi."

"You are not speaking the truth," said Owen. "How can he be a Copt and bring money to be given to a Moslem for the Moslem to use against the Copts?"

"I do not know what use he makes of it, effendi," said Mordecai humbly.

"Are you sure the bringer is a Copt?"

"Yes, effendi."

Mordecai spoke with certainty; and indeed, it was something which no Cairene would have been uncertain on.

"The other bearer," said Georgiades, "the first one, the one who was but a servant, was he also a Copt?"

"An Armenian, effendi."

No help there, and in fact there was little more help to be had from Mordecai at all. They told him to keep his mouth shut and left, not by the way they had come but through another door which led out through the bazaar.

"A Copt?" said Owen. "I can't understand it."

"Maybe someone's just being clever," said Georgiades.

"I've found something new at any rate," said Mahmoud.

They were sitting at an outside table in one of the corner cafés of the Ataba el-Khadra, out of reach of the traffic but strategically placed so that they could watch not only all the interesting things that went on in the square but also the more sophisticated exchanges which went on between tourist and native in Musky Street. It had been a long, hard day and Owen would have quite liked a whisky. However, in deference to his friend's Moslem susceptibilities he had stayed with coffee, and certainly Turkish coffee taken *mazbout,* sweetened, was perfectly to his taste.

"Anything useful?"

"It might be. Someone's turned up who claims that Zoser had a visitor the night before he killed the Zikr."

"Why the hell didn't he turn up before?"

"Because he's been away. He travels with camels and has just got back. When he got back his sister told him. He stays with her between trips. She lives in the house next to the Zosers. That's where he was that night. They remembered it because it was so unusual for the Zosers to have a visitor, and because he came so late. They had already put the beds down and had to move them."

"Why didn't she say anything?"

"Thought it wasn't for a woman, etc. She had no man to go for her—her husband was away travelling too—so she waited for her brother to get back."

"Does she corroborate?"

"Yes, they both remember."

"Any details?"

"Not many. Nothing to identify by. It was dark and it was

late, so late that the lamps had already been put out, they hardly saw him, you know, all that sort of thing."

"Real, or are they saying that just to keep out of trouble?"

"If they wanted to keep out of trouble they wouldn't have bothered to have come to the police station."

"True. So you've nothing to go by?"

"Except that he was a Copt."

"Even in the dark they would know that."

"I take it, from the fact that they remarked on it, that they're not Copt themselves?"

"You take it correctly. They're Moslem."

"How did they get on with the Zosers? Friends? Enemies?"

"So-so. Nothing much. Hardly saw each other. The Zosers kept pretty much to themselves. Didn't have much to do with anybody. That's why they remembered that night."

"Hear anything?"

"Nothing they could repeat. Except that he was clearly not a stranger."

Owen sipped his coffee.

"Pity there's nothing more," he said. "It could be significant."

"Of course there's someone else who could tell."

"There is?"

"You're forgetting Zoser's wife. She was there."

"The one with the hand-painting? Yes, I'd forgotten about her."

"She would know. The only thing is, she's moved. In fact, that's what I wanted to ask you. I don't suppose you've any idea where I could find her?"

"As a matter of fact," said Owen, remembering Georgiades's visit to the funeral, "I think I have."

They almost missed the man when at last he came. Mordecai had said that he usually approached the shop through the bazaar, and that was the side they had been watching. There were several little alleyways that he might have used and they had a man watching each one; but then in the end he approached from the other side, not through the bazaar at all but along through the streets, the way they themselves had come on that previous visit. Georgiades had a man on that route too, but there was only one of him and when he saw the man coming he did not risk leaving his post to run and tell them but watched the man until he was safely inside the shop.

They had wondered about concealing themselves in the shop itself, in the recess possibly, but had decided not to risk it. The aim, after all, was not to arrest the man but to follow him and see if by that means they could uncover the line which ran back from Mordecai's shop to the ultimate suppliers of Osman's money.

Instead, they had taken up position in one of the shops opposite where they were concealed by heavy wooden boarding and from where they could see directly into Mordecai's shop. They saw the man come in from the street and stand for a moment adjusting to the darkness. They caught a glimpse of his robe in the candlelight, but only a glimpse because then he moved into the shadows and it was only by Mordecai's gestures that they could tell where he was.

Somebody slid into the shop beside them. It was their agent.

"It is him, effendi. I saw him clearly, but I dared not move. It is the one we were told to expect."

"He had a bag with him?"

"Yes, effendi. As the Jew said."

"Good. Go back now in case he leaves by the way he came. If he does, follow him until the tracker takes over."

Owen had borrowed for the day some skilled police trackers, men who could follow a trail, or a man, even through the crowded streets of Cairo. He did not want anything to go wrong.

The agent slipped away unobtrusively.

In the shop opposite, Mordecai appeared to be bowing farewell. He straightened up, came to the front of the shop and stood for a moment looking out impassively. Then he moved aside, and a man came out of the darkness of the shop, hesitated for a fraction of a second and then turned away into the bazaar.

Owen stood for a moment in stunned shock.

The man was Andrus.

CHAPTER 11

"I don't understand it," said Owen flatly.

"Me neither," said Georgiades.

"I thought he was the man behind the organization on the Coptic side."

"Well," said Nikos, "he is. I don't think there is any doubt about it."

"Then why the hell is he the man behind the Moslem organization too?"

"He's not exactly that, surely," Nikos objected.

"He supplies the money, doesn't he? And without that the Moslems wouldn't be half as effective."

"They're not paying him interest, are they? I mean, he's not doing it for money?"

"Osman? Pay interest? To a Copt?"

"Funnier things have happened. Like a Copt lending money to Osman."

"Osman personally doesn't have money enough even to pay the interest," said Nikos.

"Friends?"

"We're back to them again. And the only friend that's appeared so far is Andrus."

"Maybe he is a friend. In secret, I mean."

"Of the Moslems? Of Osman? I don't mind us looking at some funny ideas," said Georgiades, "but let's not go crazy."

"That can't be it," said Nikos.

"No. Well, I'm not really suggesting that it is. I'm just reviewing all the possibilities."

"While you're doing that," said Nikos, "think about this one: Andrus doesn't know what the money is being used for."

"That it's going straight to Osman? He set it up, didn't he?"

"Well, did he? It was set up that way, certainly, but was it set up by him?"

"He's involved."

"Oh yes, he's involved. But does he know?"

"Someone else set it up and he's just being used?"

"It's a possibility."

"OK. I'll acknowledge it as a possibility."

"I've got another question," said Georgiades. "If he's a secret friend of the Moslems, why doesn't he just give them the money directly. Why does he have to go through Mordecai?"

"I can answer that one," said Owen. "He's had to go through Mordecai precisely because he is a Copt. The Moslems wouldn't accept it if it came straight from him."

"They think it comes from other Moslems?"

"Possibly. I can't see Osman accepting it otherwise."

"Well, I find it confusing," said Georgiades. "I thought it was all straightforward, with Moslems cutting Copts' throats, as they have always done, and Copts cutting Moslems' throats, as usual. Now it's got more complicated."

"Let's go back to basics," said Owen. "First, are we wrong about Andrus being behind it all on the Copt side?"

"No!" said Nikos.

He went to his desk and produced a sheaf of agents' reports.

"If you look at my map," he said with a tinge of pride, "you will see that all the incidents are still within half a mile of the Bab es Zuweyla. Not only that, they're not spontaneous, they're organized. After each incident the men go back and report. I've had them followed. They always go to the same place. It's a house just behind the Mar Girgis. It belongs to the church and is used by its laymen for committees and administering charity. The church has a large charity programme. Anyway, that's where they all go to report. Not only that; that's where they get their instructions, because sometimes some of them go out again for a second time to take part in another incident. I've had my people watching the house for some time now. That's where they report before they start and that's where they report after they're finished."

"Why don't we smash it up?"

"Because then they'd report somewhere else. Anyway, I thought you wanted to be sure about who was organizing it."

"I do. Who is?"

"It's got to be Andrus. There are other people in the house

from time to time, but he's the only one who has been there throughout."

"You haven't been able to get anyone inside?"

"No, but I probably could. Do you want me to?"

"Yes. Let's have some certainty about one thing, at any rate."

"Why don't we pick a few of them up," said Georgiades, "as they're going to and fro? Then we could ask them."

"We could do that too. I've thought about it," said Nikos, "but I was keeping to surveillance until I was told otherwise."

Nikos was a stickler for the rules. Owen never ceased to marvel at the way in which he combined incredible ingenuity within the rules with total lack of curiosity as to what went on beyond them.

"You mean you've known all along where they were going?" asked Georgiades.

"Not till they got there. I've known they were going, that's all."

"And you've done nothing about it?"

"Of course I've done something about it. I've had them followed from the time they left the house. The moment it was clear where they were going I've had a message back. And then," said Nikos with pride, "I've had our people there within minutes. That's organization."

"Yes, but it's all unnecessary. You could have hit them the moment they left the house."

"Can't do that."

"Why not?"

"Because we're still on surveillance."

"Christ!"

"Other reasons too," Owen intervened. "There's no point in picking up small fry. Not when there are so many of them. It's big fry we're after."

"If you'd been out on the street"—Georgiades looked at Nikos—"instead of sitting on your ass in a cool office—"

"What I do," said Nikos, "takes ability."

"How did you get onto it in the first place?" Owen asked curiously.

"I had them followed back. After the first few incidents I began to suspect there was a pattern, so I tried to find it. You don't get anything on this scale without communication lines, so I started looking for them."

"Have you got it all worked out for the Moslems too?" asked Georgiades. "It's not that I mind wasting my time, it's just that I like to know that I'm wasting my time."

"You're not wasting your time," said Owen pacifically.

"It's not as clear-cut on the Moslem side," said Nikos, "not as well organized. There's no reporting back, for instance, so they don't know how well they've done or what mistakes they make. But instructions have to be given, so again there are lines of communication."

"Which you're shadowing?"

Nikos nodded.

"They don't always work. Some of the incidents are spontaneous. The other thing is that they have a general idea of what Osman wants so they don't bother about instructions, they just go out and do it."

"I think I may be a secret Moslem," Georgiades said to Owen. "You didn't know that, did you?"

"It all comes from Osman, does it?" asked Owen.

"Yes, Osman and Andrus. They're the two."

"They're the one if it all comes back to Andrus."

Georgiades went to the door and called for Yussuf. One of the other bearers shouted back encouragingly. In Yussuf's present numb state they had taken to covering for him.

Owen sat there thinking. He couldn't make any sense of it. The premise that everything started from was Andrus's hostility to anything Moslem. It had been there right from the beginning, right from the night of the dog. It ran through everything. It had never wavered. He could not believe that it was wavering now. But how else to explain his actions? The money was definitely being brought to Mordecai; and Mordecai was definitely passing it on to Osman. Not only that; Mordecai was equally definite that he was merely doing as he had been instructed. And Owen believed him.

Andrus was part of it. About that there could be no doubt. But how extensive a part? Might Nikos be right and Andrus merely an unwitting accomplice, ignorant of for whom the money was intended? But then, Nikos was himself a Copt and, yes, under an obligation to Andrus; might not he be biased in

Andrus's favour? And then again, for all his brilliance at organization, Nikos sometimes overdid the speculation.

"Try another idea," said Nikos. "Why don't you apply the analysis you made of the Moslems to the Copts?"

"What analysis?"

"The political connection. You know, that there was a group of people at the top, ministers, perhaps, who had an interest in keeping relations between Copts and Moslems on the boil. You thought that might lie behind Mahmoud being brought back into the Zoser case. Keep the wound open. Copts against Moslems. I liked that analysis. It avoided the mistake that is so often made. People assume, the British especially, who appear to have a unique talent for combining sentimentality and intellectual evasion, that conflict, even massacre, is in no one's interest. But they're wrong. Sometimes it is in someone's interest. And then if you want to find out the reason for the tension or how to stop it, what you have to do is look at the interests of those concerned. Perhaps the mistake we have been making is in applying that thinking to the Moslems but not to the Copts."

Owen reached out his hand for the coffee a bearer had just brought in. A different bearer. Not Yussuf.

"Applying it, then, to the Copts," said Owen, "what do we get?"

"Someone on the Coptic side wants to keep things on the boil, wants to stop agreement from being reached. To do that, they're even prepared to give money to Moslems."

"To be used against Copts?"

"All the more effective," said Nikos, "if you wanted to keep things on the boil."

Georgiades put his mug back on the tray.

"Someone's a clever bastard," he said. "Of course, it may just be you."

"It fits," said Owen. "It explains the money."

"Not only that."

"Yes," said Owen. "It explains Andrus too."

One of the bearers rushed into the office.

"Effendi! Come quickly. Yussuf has taken a knife!"

Owen ran down the corridor and into the bearers' room. There were shocked faces everywhere but no Yussuf.

"Where is he?"

"He ran out, effendi. He said he would kill them."

"Who?"

"Suleiman, effendi. And Fatima."

One of the bearers plucked at his arm.

"He took my knife, effendi. He took my knife."

"Where is Suleiman's house?"

It was in the bazaar area.

"Take me there."

The man ran out with Owen on his heels. Two of the other bearers followed.

From the Bab el-Khalkh to the Bab es Zuweyla was about half a mile. A man would go faster than an arabeah, certainly if you took into account the time needed to explain it to the arabeah driver. The bearer set off along the wide, dusty street. He was one of the younger bearers and ran fast. Owen found it hard to keep up with him. Within a minute the sweat was pouring off him and his jacket sticking to his back.

The bearer slowed to let him come up with him.

"Run on!" said Owen. "Fast."

This was how they could save time, catch up. Once they were through the Gate they wouldn't be able to run at all. The streets would be too crowded.

The bearer drew away again. He was running barefoot and had the advantage over Owen in his heavy shoes. By the time they had reached the Gate he was a dozen or more yards ahead.

Owen dashed up almost blinded with sweat.

"On! Get on!" he managed to gasp.

The bearer plunged at once into the warren of tiny streets, alleyways and passages between stalls that made up the area loosely known as the bazaars. Every road, every lane, even the narrowest of alleys was taken up with stalls. And wherever there was a stall, inevitably the passage was blocked by the wares which spread out from it, covering the ground on all sides, stretching right across the thoroughfare so that there was indeed no thoroughfare but you had to pick your way among pots and pans, saddles, boots, baskets, melons, bales of cloth, onions, and canvases appliquéd with texts from the Koran and crude copies of the tomb-paintings of the pharaohs.

And wherever there was a suggestion of a space there

would be a craftsman bent over his work: a weaver over his loom, a metal-worker crouched over a dish of grey ash fanning a lump of live charcoal in its midst with a blowpipe, a basket-worker holding what he was making with his toes so as to leave his hands free, a turner doing his turning with a little bow which might have been used to shoot arrows, the man making pegs for the ornate wooden windows.

Owen was in despair. Not only could he find no space to put even one foot, but whenever he hesitated, hands reached up at him beckoning him to buy. He slowed almost to a halt.

The bearer kept looking back at him. Owen would have told the man to run on but without him he would have been lost at once. What had happened to the two other bearers who had started out with them he did not know.

The bearer pulled him into a passage so thin that even the narrowest of stalls could not wedge itself in. There was barely space for a person to pass. Halfway along they met a woman. She pushed herself back against the wall to avoid touching a man but as Owen pressed past her he was as conscious of her roundnesses and softnesses as if he had been in bed beside her.

They came out into a slightly wider passage where there were no stalls but children were playing and black-gowned women standing in doorways talking. They looked up at him in surprise and pulled their veils back across their faces. One or two snatched up their children and held them close, making signs to warn off the evil eye. This was mediaeval Cairo, mediaeval still.

They went up another narrow passageway, not so much a passage as a mere slit between houses, and came out suddenly into open space. After the darkness and coolness the light and heat struck him like a blow.

The bearer looked round. Everywhere was rubble. There wasn't a single building standing for hundreds of yards. The ground was covered with crumbling mud-bricks, heaps of cracked white stone. A dog barked and was answered by another. Out in the rubble he saw others skulking.

Then he realized where they were: the Coptic Place of the Dead.

The bearer turned left along a line of houses they had just come out of. The big ones they had passed through gave way to smaller, two-storey ones built of mud-brick which the rains were gradually dissolving. Everything was crumbling, falling down. Here and there were gaps in the line where houses had collapsed completely.

There was a piercing whistle and a little boy ran across the rubble towards them.

"Effendi! Effendi!"

It was the boy he had met when Georgiades had taken him back to the Place of the Dead; Ali, Yussuf's nephew.

"This way!"

He raced off across the rubble. Owen stumbled behind him, his feet sliding and tripping on the loose stones.

They came to a blank white stuccoed wall. Owen stopped abruptly. The boy had completely disappeared.

"Effendi! Here!"

To his left an urgent face, an arm beckoning. He ran across.

"Under here!"

There was a gap in the lower part of the wall big enough for a boy, hardly big enough for a man to squeeze through. He forced his way through it. They were in what had been a walled garden and was now just a mass of rubble. Ali turned immediately to his right and climbed over a broken-down wall. They were in another disused, rubble-filled space which might once have been a yard or garden.

Ali ran to the next wall.

"Effendi! Quickly!"

"Is he there?"

"Yes, but they have barred the door."

Owen found a hole in the wall, used it as a stepping place and swung his leg over the top. Then he stopped.

Below him was another space which had once been a courtyard. It was filled now with heaps of brick and stone. These had perhaps once been outhouses which had long ago fallen down. Piles of rubble lay against the side of the house. There had once been an outside staircase leading up to the flat roof but that too had collapsed. There was a mud brick wall round the roof of the house, over which looked two agitated faces, those of a man and a woman. The wall was crumbling and there were great gaps in it. It offered no defence; and defence was needed, for on the opposite side of the yard a wall ran right up to the house and although it was lower than the roof an agile man might easily scramble from it up onto the roof itself. And along the wall a man was climbing. Yussuf.

"Yussuf!"

Yussuf stopped, startled. He looked round, saw Owen and hesitated.

"Yussuf! Come down at once."

Yussuf almost started to obey. Then he shook his head and began to climb determinedly on. In between his teeth he was holding a huge knife.

The wall was narrow and missing many of its bricks. It was not easy to climb along it and he had to go slowly. He needed both hands as well as his toes.

Owen called again but Yussuf ignored him. The faces on the roof disappeared and then appeared again. A woman began screaming.

Owen threw himself over the wall and dropped down. He had hoped to find a door. There was one but it was blocked up. There was no other way in which he could get up to the roof.

"Have you a gun, effendi?"

He shook his head. He never carried one unless there was a special reason why he might have to use it. He would never have thought of bringing it out against Yussuf.

He looked round for a stick or prop which he could use to dislodge Yussuf. There wasn't one. Wood was as scarce as silver in the poorer parts of Cairo.

He seized a brick desperately and threw it at Yussuf. It hit the wall four feet below him. Ali threw, more accurately. The brick hit Yussuf and jolted him but he shrugged it aside. The top of the wall was in better repair closer to the house and he scurried along it.

He had almost reached the house when another brick hit him. It would have struck him in the face if at the last moment, sensing it coming, he had not ducked his head. The movement threw him off balance. A brick beneath him crumbled and suddenly the whole wall began to sag. Yussuf tried to recover his balance, tried to jump, but the wall collapsed too fast. It subsided in a great cloud of dust. Yussuf was pitched off onto the other side. They heard the heavy thud as he fell.

Owen ran across. The dust was so thick that for a moment

he could not see. Then, below him on the rubble, he made out Yussuf's motionless body.

And beyond him, for some strange reason, on the other side of the neighbouring courtyard, was a totally amazed and bemused Mahmoud.

Owen slid down into the courtyard in a small shower of mud and masonry.

There was a woman standing beside Mahmoud. She had thrown her hands up over her face in shock. He could see the hands very clearly; well enough to notice the hand-painting.

"What the hell is this?" said Mahmoud. He rarely swore.

"My bearer," said Owen briefly.

He knelt beside Yussuf. There was an ugly wound on his head. If he breathed it was imperceptible.

Ali came across and touched Yussuf with his foot.

"He is not dead," he said.

Ali was an expert on such matters.

The woman brought water from the house, knelt down beside Yussuf and began to mop his wound. Ali went and sat in the shade.

Owen went across to Mahmoud.

"What's she doing here?" He motioned to the woman kneeling beside Yussuf.

"Don't you remember? You told me."

"Christ, is this where she lives?"

"Where she lives now. She's moved, if you remember."

"Have you talked to her?"

"I *was* talking to her."

"Did you find out anything?"

"Not much. A man certainly came that night but it was to see her, not her husband."

"That late?"

"She wouldn't see him before. It wouldn't have been proper to have seen him alone. Her husband was out."

"So the man waited till he got back?"

"He knew he would be late. Zoser was at the church."

"Zoser says. She says. It would be worth checking."

"It's easily checked. Zoser occasionally stayed late to help with the charity dispensation. She was involved with that too. That was what the man came to see her about. There were some women he wanted her to take relief to. She often did that, she says. Of course, the men couldn't go to the women themselves."

"Did the man talk to her husband?"

"She doesn't think so."

The woman went into the house to get some water. Yussuf was beginning to stir. Mahmoud went across and picked the knife up out of the rubble.

Ali had been listening to the discussion.

"I know that woman," he said.

"How do you know her?"

"She was at the house that night. The night of the dog."

"The house of Andrus?"

"Yes."

"She is a relative of Andrus?"

"No, no." Ali was shocked that anyone could make a mistake so gross.

"She was there to cry."

Owen thought he understood. She must be a professional mourner. When a significant person died, women were sometimes hired to weep during the funeral ceremonies.

"Andrus paid her?"

"No," said the woman, returning with the water. "No one paid me. Much. I do it out of friendship."

"For Andrus?"

"Not for him especially. I do it for all of the community. Other families were in the Place of the Dead that night. I was with Sesostris. He sent me to Andrus in the early part of the night because he knew Andrus lacked women."

"In the early part of the night? Did you go past the tomb of Andrus?"

"Yes."

"Did you see anything untoward?"

"Only the shadows," said the woman. "I saw the shadows and was frightened. It is the night that the spirits return."

"And did you see them about the tomb?"

"Yes, and I was frightened and hurried on. When I reached the house of Andrus I spoke of it to the other women and we said a prayer. And when I left, I looked again, and there were no shadows, so I knew our prayer had been heard."

"That was in the morning? Before the dawn?"

"No. It was in the middle of the night. I had to mourn for Sesostris so I went back to his house."

"You only spent part of the night with Andrus?"

"The early part. Then I went to Sesostris. And then at dawn I went to Zakatellos. I had promised him I would be there for the visit."

She bent over Yussuf and splashed water on his face. He opened his eyes, saw her and struggled to sit up.

"Away, woman!" he said. "I have no need of Copts."

"You have a need of someone," she said, "whoever it be."

"Was your husband with you?" asked Owen.

"No. He was keeping vigil at the church."

"And you were at the houses. Were you with Andrus when he went to the tomb?"

"No."

"So you did not know about the dog?"

"Not till later. I was with Sesostris when one ran and told us."

"And you told your husband?"

"When I got home."

"And did he speak with Andrus?"

"Not then. Later. When Andrus came to visit me."

"Thank you," said Owen.

"I've done the checking you wanted," said Georgiades, "and it's not been easy, I can tell you. I went first to his business premises. It's not a bad little business. He does all right. Nothing huge, small to medium. Nowhere near big enough for him to finance the war on his own, especially as he gives such a lot to charity. And he does give it to charity. There's no doubt about that. I've talked to his personal clerk. Steady sums, increasing over the years as he's become more pious. The clerk is secretary to the charity programme of the church and knows the recipients."

"Zoser?"

"I don't think so. Not in money. In kind, perhaps. Favours, maybe. He does people quite a lot of those."

"And they do him some. Go back to the money. Does he finance the charitable programme himself?"

"The church's? No, they all chip in. Andrus put in a fair amount but bigger boys give more."

"OK. So after living expenses and charity there's not a lot left over. Not enough to finance all the agitation on the Coptic side, let alone the Moslems as well."

"Nowhere near enough."

"So the money he gives to Osman must come from somewhere else. Does he have a bank for his business or does he just use cash?"

"He's got to have a bank. His business is international, remember. He sometimes needs quite sophisticated credit arrangements."

"Do you know which one?"

"Yes. He is a small businessman and he likes to deal with small bankers. They've got to be Coptic, of course, and preferably someone he's met through the church. He goes to Sesostris."

"So he could be getting the money there?"

"Don't rush me. Next, I checked on his movements on Fridays. That's the day, remember, when he takes the money to Mordecai. It's the Moslem Sabbath, of course, so a good day for Copts to do business on. Well, it's hard to check the whole day, as you can imagine. But that is the day, it appears, when he regularly goes to his own bank. He's been doing it for years. So far as I can tell, and that's not as far as I'd like, on the last few Fridays he's not been going to any other bank or finance house. Nor is there any single person whom he's been visiting regularly."

"Anyone come to see him?"

"Not at the business. Nor at home, as far as I can tell from his servants. Possibly at the church house, where, as you know, he's been spending a lot of time recently."

"So it could very well be the bank?"

"That's what I thought too. So then I went to the bank and asked politely in the name of the Mamur Zapt if I could check Andrus's account. Sesostris said no."

"He can't say no. Not if it's the Mamur Zapt."

"Well, I said it was the Mamur Zapt and he said no. He wants proper legal notification."

"I'll bloody notify him. Deliver it personally. In the cell."

"He's an awkward bugger. Andrus and he are two of a kind.

Difficult sods, both. However, mere refusal does not stop me. I talked to the tellers. They said yes, Andrus did come on Fridays and had been doing so for years. Any especially big drawings lately? Well, they said, they wouldn't know, since he always went straight in to Sesostris. Again, his pattern for years. No change here. Also it's the way the bank works. Sesostris does it all personally. The Copts like that. It's always man-to-man stuff with them. Funny, considering how they also like to put it all down on paper."

"Are you saying Sesostris hands over the cash personally?"

"No. The cashier does that. Andrus just pops in to see Sesostris and they have a bit of a chat, not a long one, they don't even have a cup of coffee, mean bastards, both of them, and then Andrus goes on to the cashier presumably with Sesostris's authorization and the cashier takes the money out of the safe and gives it to him. I tried to have a word with the cashier but he wasn't talking. More than his job's worth, I suppose, though these Copts are always tight-mouthed as well as tight-fisted. Well, not all of them. I got something out of the tellers. One of them said that Andrus normally took his money away in a small bag, one he could conceal under his gown, it's safer that way. But for the last week or two he's had to use a bigger bag. The charity programme's been growing. Actually it has, though whether by enough to require a bigger bag I haven't been able to make out."

"It would be interesting to see the account."

"That wouldn't tell you much. It will either show he's overdrawn or that money has been credited. If it's been credited, then the only person who will be able to tell you where it comes from is Sesostris."

"Is he involved, do you think? Personally, I mean?"

"They're all involved. You see, the way the Copts work is that if they decide on something, like a campaign of trouble-making and agitation, the first thing they do is set up an organization. Then they set up resourcing arrangements, just as they would do for any other business operation they undertook. They would arrange drawing facilities, appoint a local agent, etc. Sesostris may be just another mechanism, like Mordecai."

"Like Andrus?"

"Could be. The local agent. On the other hand, if you were

Andrus and for some reason you decided to start a campaign of your own, and you were, like him, a Copt, the first thing you would do would be to go to a bank and make proper financial arrangements. And when I say proper, I mean proper. You wouldn't go to anyone else, because banks are where you go for finance, and you wouldn't go to a shady one, because that's not sound business practise."

"You think he might be doing it on his own?"

Georgiades hesitated.

"Well, it could be. He's strong enough, he's got a grudge, he's doing something about it. He's the one who's actually masterminding the campaign."

"I agree with all that," said Owen. "But."

"But what?"

"Remember what Nikos said: apply the analysis not to the Moslems but to the Copts. Not Osman, but Osman plus money. Not Andrus, but Andrus plus money. Where does it come from?"

"Sympathizers. There are a lot of Copts who agree with him. They're subscribing."

"Using the bank as a collecting point? Well, you might be right. But I'm sticking with the analysis."

"Test it out," Georgiades invited. "Talk to him."

"Andrus? I might just do that."

"After all," said Georgiades, "you've got an excuse."

"What?"

"Zoser. He talked to Zoser the night before the killing. Remember?"

Mahmoud leaned forward in his chair. Since it was ostensibly in connection with the Zoser case, it was his business, and they met in his office.

"So on that night," he said, "the night before the Zikr was killed, you talked only about the money she was to give out?"

"Why do you ask me these questions?" asked Andrus. "What have I to do with the Zikr?"

"You talked only about the money she was to give out?"

"Yes. As I said."

"Did you have any money with you?"

"No. It is best not to carry money in Cairo at night. She was to collect it from the church house in the morning."

"Where you would give it her?"

"Yes."

"Did you give it her?"

"Of course."

"Personally?"

"Yes. I was there when she came."

"You are there a lot," said Owen, "these days."

It was the first time he had spoken. Andrus gave him a hostile look.

"Yes. I am. The church has a considerable charity programme which I administer. There is nothing wrong with that, surely?"

"Not with that, no."

"You talked that night about the people she was to give the money to," said Mahmoud. "Their names?"

"Their names?"

"Yes. Could you tell me the names, please."

"Why should I tell you their names? What business is it of yours?"

"I need to know them."

"I forget them."

Mahmoud sighed and made a note with his pencil. He would check the names with the woman. If there were any names.

"You talked with the woman," he said. "Did you also talk with her husband?"

"With Zoser?"

"Yes, Zoser."

"Whom you killed," said Andrus, looking at Owen.

"He killed himself. And someone else."

Andrus looked as if he was going to say something, then changed his mind.

"Answer my question!" said Mahmoud.

Andrus looked at him with undisguised fury. Owen suddenly remembered that Mahmoud was a Moslem.

"Of course I talked to him," said Andrus.

"What about?"

"How can I remember?"

"Did you talk to him about what happened at your father's tomb?"

"I may have done. I do not know."

"And what was his response?"

Andrus did not reply. He seemed to be looking into space. Perhaps it was the reference to his father's tomb. Owen suddenly felt unexpectedly sorry for him. It came home to him for the first time that what had seemed to him a trivial event, a stupid joke, was something genuinely much bigger to Andrus. It had touched him on a raw spot. That harsh, unaccommodating man had clearly loved his father, perhaps had loved him alone. Owen felt a twinge of pity.

"And what was his response?" Mahmoud prompted softly.

Andrus came back from space and looked at him bitterly.

"I do not know why I should tell you," he said. "However, I will tell you. He was shocked and horrified. He felt for me as would anyone of a right mind. And then he was angry. That this should happen to one he knew and an elder of the church. At first he could not comprehend it. But then he realized. This blow was not aimed at me but at the Church. It was struck not at the weak man who suffered it but at the strong God who was the man's master. And he said to himself: 'That man is weak indeed who lets his master suffer such an insult. We looked for redress from the Mamur Zapt and received none. But that was right. We were wrong to look for redress from others when we should be taking the wrong done to our master upon ourselves.' That was Zoser's response."

"That was what you told him," said Owen.

"That was what he said," said Andrus.

And almost certainly believed it. When he had finished he sat glaring at them in defiance and pride. Owen could believe that he had poured out all the wound and hurt that was in his heart when he spoke to Zoser. And he could believe that although Zoser might not have said these things he had actually felt them. And if he had felt them, might have done something about them.

Had Andrus intended that Zoser should do something about them?

"You told him these things," said Owen, "in order to inflame him."

"I did not."

"You killed Zoser," said Owen. "Not I."

For the barest second Andrus seemed to flinch. Then the moment passed and the certainty returned.

"God is great," said Andrus, "and will not desert his servant."

"There is a law of man, too," said Mahmoud, "and that too must be obeyed."

He probed on, and Owen was glad, for it gave him time to think. He needed to think, because although he was sure that Andrus had been speaking the truth, and that he had not deliberately incited Zoser to kill, he still felt puzzled. If everything he had projected onto Zoser was true, or a true picture of his own feelings, why had he not taken the action upon himself?

As Mahmoud continued with his patient questions, and Andrus continued with his impatient replies, an answer began to come to him. Andrus, for all his faults, was, politics aside (and no Egyptian would accept that politics had anything to do with morality), a moral man. He would not kill. On the other hand, his wound went so deep and he was such a vengeful man that he had wanted his wounder dead. When he had spoken to Zoser something of this had come across, perhaps not consciously but perhaps not completely unconsciously either. He had said it speaking what he believed to be truth and justice, said it and left it. If Zoser picked it up, then that was God's will. If Zoser did not pick it up, then that was God's will. There had been an act but he, Andrus, had not acted. He had done nothing inconsistent with his morality.

Listening to Andrus now, Owen felt again his immense moral rigidity. He had to have absolute certainty. There was no room for doubt, least of all self-doubt. Mahmoud's barbs, and there were plenty of them now, for Mahmoud was getting irritated, bounced off his massive self-assurance like wooden arrows off a rock of granite.

If they were going to get anywhere with Andrus, not on the Zoser business, Owen was satisfied about that, but on the other, then that granite surface must be undermined. Somehow or other they had to get beneath the certainty and feed the seeds of doubt.

"Tell me, Andrus," said Owen, "why do you spend all day and every day at the church house?"

"I am doing God's work," said Andrus, caught rather off guard.

"Are you sure that God would own it?"

There was a little silence.

"Why should he not own it?"

Owen did not reply, merely waited.

"God loves charity," said Andrus, with slightly less than his usual self-assurance.

"No doubt, but what is that to do with what you are doing?"

"What are you accusing me of? Why don't you speak out?" Andrus began to grow angry. "Do you think I am frightened of you?"

Owen took no notice.

"You are spending a lot of time there," he said almost conversationally. "Have you given up your business?"

"My business is no concern of yours."

"I thought you might have given it up. You spend so much time at the church house."

"Have you been spying on me?"

"I would have thought you needed the money."

"My business is doing well," said Andrus, "and I have no need of money."

"For what you are doing at the church house, I mean," Owen explained.

"I give to charity what I can afford."

"Yes, but the other things."

"What other things?"

"The other things you do at the church house."

"I do not know what you mean," said Andrus. "I do God's work."

"Oh no. God is a god of peace."

Andrus was brought up short. After a moment he said to Owen:

"You are mistaken. He is a god of war. Ask him." He pointed to Mahmoud. "He is a Moslem and will tell you."

Mahmoud looked uncomfortable.

"God is a god of neither peace nor war," he said. "It is man who makes war and man who makes peace."

Andrus stood up.

"Are you going to take me?" he said to Owen.

"Perhaps."

"I am not frightened of you."

"Why should you be," asked Owen, "when all you will get is justice?"

"Your justice."

"Egyptian justice."

"Does a Copt ever get justice," asked Andrus, "in Egypt?" He turned impatiently towards the door. "Come! Take me!"

"Sit down!"

If he took Andrus now it would be no good. The Copts would merely regroup without him. And Andrus would be untouched, impregnable behind his rigid simplicities. His world was still certain.

"Why do the British hate the Copts?" asked Andrus.

"We do not hate the Copts. We are neutral between Copts and Moslems."

"How can a Christian be a Christian and be neutral?"

"We are all servants of the Khedive," said Owen, correct in form if not in substance, "British as well as Copt, Copt as well as Moslem."

"I do not understand," said Andrus, "how a Christian can voluntarily choose to serve a Moslem."

"Many do," Owen pointed out, "including many Copts."

For some reason this seemed to irritate Andrus particularly.

"They are traitors!" he said passionately. "They are traitors to the Coptic cause."

"To try to provide good government to the people of Egypt is hardly to be a traitor."

"The people of Egypt! Who are the people of Egypt? We are. The Copts. And for two thousand years we have had a government not our own. And why is that? Because we Copts have let others govern us. We have even helped them to govern. We have worked with the Government when we should have been working against it. For two thousand years we have done that. And for two thousand years every government has been that of an invader."

Where had he heard that before?

"You are a Moslem," Andrus said to Mahmoud, "and you

are an invader. You are invaders too," he said to Owen, "but you are Christian. When the British came we thought that they would lift the Moslem yoke from off our backs. But Christian turned against Christian. They supported the Moslems instead of sweeping them away."

The moment of doubt, if there had been one, had gone. Andrus was back in his old self-confident stride. He would go to prison, if he had to go to prison, convinced of his rightness, proud of his martyrdom.

It was time to move in.

"Andrus," said Owen, "you surprise me. You hate the Moslems. Why then do you support them?"

Andrus stopped.

"Support them?"

"Yes. Against your own people, too."

"I don't know what you mean," Andrus declared flatly.

"Sheikh Osman. You give him money."

"Nonsense!"

"All the money that Sheikh Osman has used in the past few weeks in his war against the Copts is money that you have given him."

"Nonsense!" said Andrus. "I have given him no money. How would I give him money? You invent these things to trick me."

"Every week," said Owen, "every Friday, you take money to Mordecai."

"Well," said Andrus, "what of it?"

"Which he gives to Osman."

"That is just a lie," said Andrus. "Why do you bother with such tricks?"

"I will bring Mordecai to you if you wish, and he will confirm what I say."

"You have told him what to say."

"I will show you the evidence that Osman goes to him every Friday and comes away with the money you have given him."

"But—but this cannot be."

"All the money that has been used against the Copts has been supplied by you. And you talk of traitors!"

"Mordecai is the traitor. How dare he do this thing?"

"He does only what he has been told."

"The money was brought for another purpose."

"What purpose, Andrus?"

Andrus was silent.

"You brought the money, Andrus, and gave it to Mordecai to be used against the Copts. Against your own people. Why did you do that, Andrus?"

"I did not bring it for that purpose," said Andrus hoarsely. "Mordecai has tricked me."

"Not Mordecai. It is not Mordecai who has tricked you. Mordecai has only carried out instructions. Whose instructions were they, Andrus? If they were not yours, whose were they?"

Andrus would not reply.

CHAPTER 12

The Mamur Zapt sat in his office, thinking. Nikos started to come into the room, stopped and withdrew unobserved. No one after that was allowed past the office. The bearers sensed the situation and stayed quietly in their office at the other end of the corridor. They were in any case somewhat subdued by Yussuf's misfortunes. A sympathetic peace descended on the corridor.

In fact, Owen was thinking mostly about Zeinab. Since their visit to the opera relations between them had been distinctly cool, and Owen was feeling the effects of being deprived. He had decided that it was time to think things through and settle them once and for all, but whenever he started thinking about Zeinab thoughts became memories of touch and smell and look and emotion and he became most unsettled. He had to admit, too, that a certain drama had gone out of his life. He considered himself on the whole a pretty steady person, but the trouble with steadiness was that it could very easily become the humdrum. Zeinab, whatever else she might be, was definitely not humdrum. She had all an Arab's volatility, added to which was an emphatic unpredictability which was all her own. Too strong-willed and forceful to remain easily in any slot into which a male-oriented Moslem society might force her, regarding marriage, certainly to a Moslem, as the ultimate form of prison, conducting life as a ceaseless battle for Home Rule and Independence, she sometimes found things too much for her and plunged into pits of despair, from which she would spring out again almost immediately with a soar and a vehemence which left Owen dazzled. He loved her both when she was cast down and when she was leaping up, and also in between when she was normal, although as far as Zeinab was concerned normality was a flexible concept. However, "love" was, for Owen, a strong word and one which needed thinking about. Particularly in view of Paul's remarks and what he had said about Jane Postlethwaite.

Paul's remarks first. There was no need for him to get married yet. Paul's views notwithstanding, he was not old. On the other hand, Owen was uncomfortably aware, a lot of men were married. Especially senior men. You could safely disregard Paul's opinion that marriage was a prerequisite of life at the top, because Owen could think of notable exceptions, Kitchener included. Yet there was no doubt that it helped. You fitted more snugly into society, especially, the tight little society around the Consul-General, if you were married and could take your wife along to dinner parties with you, instead of forever having to be fixed up with a stray aunt or somebody. Owen did not think of himself as ambitious. He had left India for Egypt because he wanted to get out, not up. He loved his work as Mamur Zapt. It was still new to him and he wanted to go on doing it. But there might come a time, there was no denying it, when he might have had enough, and then if he wanted to move it would have to be up. But what to? That opened up whole chains of other thoughts which he put resolutely away. He had enough to think about as it was.

But the thought of possible other careers brought him to Jane Postlethwaite. There was no doubt that she would be an asset. Certainly her uncle would. An influential politician would command patronage, although one didn't like to think of it like that. Jane's husband would find ways smoothed for him, things open to him. Paul was acute on such matters. Marrying Jane Postlethwaite would be good for his career.

But what about Jane herself? She had a mind of her own

and what she wanted would in the end decide what was done. She might well reject him out of hand. It would be a very sensible thing to do and Jane Postlethwaite was a sensible girl. On the other hand, now he thought about it—that was one of the advantages of taking time out to think things through—there had been occasions when she had looked at him in a special way which made him think that she might not reject him.

However, evade and evade as he might, in the end he had to come to it: did he love Jane Postlethwaite? Enough to marry her? No, not enough to marry her, that was not it. Love her, full stop. Well, "love" was a strong word, etc., etc. Christ, he was going round in circles.

He needed some coffee.

That was another problem. He had to do something about Yussuf. Yussuf had been put in the cells to cool off and Owen had not long before been down to see him. Yussuf had been quite inconsolable.

"I have shamed the Mamur Zapt," he said. "Release me from your service! I am not worthy."

As Owen had not appointed Yussuf to his service in the first place but Yussuf had appointed himself, this seemed beside the point. However, he seemed suitably penitent, so Owen left him there while he tried to work out what to do with him.

On his way back from the cells one of the bearers had intercepted him. Yussuf's ex-wife had come to the police station and would not go away. When Owen went out to see her she was squatting in the dust of the yard, her head covered, rocking to and fro in grief.

"My man is in prison, aiee-e," she wailed.

"Be quiet, woman!" said one of the bearers. "You have caused enough trouble."

"Aiee-e," wailed the woman. "My husband has wronged the Mamur Zapt. He was bearer to the Mamur Zapt and forgot his place because of his foolish wife."

Well, that's something, at any rate, thought Owen. If Fatima was prepared to admit her foolishness something might yet be saved from the wreckage.

"Have mercy, effendi!" cried the woman, rocking to and fro.

"Have mercy and free this foolish man because of his foolish wife."

The bearers looked embarrassed and tried to get her to go. The woman shrugged off their hands and remained sitting where she was.

"Have mercy, effendi."

"I might have mercy," said Owen, "if I thought there was any point in it."

The woman stopped wailing.

"Why should there be no point in it, effendi?" she asked quietly, in a perfectly normal voice.

"Because his heart would still be troubled."

"He loves me," said the woman, slightly with surprise, slightly with satisfaction.

"He loves you and wants you back. Will you not return to him?"

The woman dropped the fold from her face and looked up at him seriously.

"I would, effendi," she said, troubled. "Suleiman is a pig. All he wants is harem business. He keeps on all the time. A little, I don't mind. It's good for a woman. But this pig thinks of nothing else."

"Yussuf is a good man," said Owen. "He has his faults, but he is a good man."

"A woman could do worse," Fatima conceded, "as I have found, unfortunately."

"Besides," said Owen, "he might have learnt his lesson."

The woman looked up at him. There was a glint in her eye.

"I think he might, effendi," she said.

"Then what is to be done?"

"Suleiman will not agree to a divorce," Fatima said, "unless you give him money. A lot of money. He thinks that because you are a good master you will want Yussuf to be happy and so will pay a lot."

"She isn't worth it," said one of the bearers firmly.

"Do not let yourself be beguiled, effendi," said another of the bearers. "Yussuf will be better off without her."

"Suleiman will tire of her," said another, "when he has had his fill."

"The Mamur Zapt has more wisdom than you," the woman retorted with spirit.

"I will think about this," Owen had said.

And thinking was what he was doing, without success.

The trouble at the bottom was money. That was another thing he had to think about. The Curbash Compensation Fund was completely exhausted. He couldn't pay for Yussuf. He couldn't pay his agents. And he certainly couldn't manage any of the substantial bribes on which the Mamur Zapt's day-to-day management of the city depended. What was he to do? Even if he survived the present crisis with its unusually heavy demands on resources, there were still a few weeks to go before he received his allocation for the next year. He would have to cut back just when spending might be most needed. There was, after all, the Moulid coming up. He would have to pay for the policing of that out of this year's money. With what?

If only John Postlethwaite would go away things could return to normal and he might be able to get some money as a special case in view of the emergency and the delicate state of politics. But what with Postlethwaite and the political situation there was absolutely no hope.

But if John Postlethwaite went he would take Jane Postlethwaite with him. Would that be a good thing or a bad thing? He was going to be leaving soon anyway so Owen would have to make up his mind about Jane. Oh Christ, there he was going round in a circle again.

Lastly, he thought about Andrus. He thought he understood now about Zoser. There had been no plot. Andrus had gone to Zoser and poured out his heart. Zoser, as rigid as Andrus and far less intelligent, had taken it upon himself to put right the wrong which had been done to his friend and his church. He could have learned who had perpetrated the deed either from Andrus or through the ordinary gossip of the bazaars. And once he had learned, for the uncomplicated Zoser there would have been no gap between decision and action.

Zoser, poor man, had seen to his own punishment. Andrus's was still to come.

Over the killing of the Zikr, Andrus, though not blameless, was probably not very guilty. On the other matter, however, inciting unrest in the city which had already led to trouble between Moslem and Copt and might still lead to massacre, Andrus was, if not *the* prime mover, then definitely *a* prime mover, and for that he must be made to pay.

But that was not what Owen was thinking about. Nor was he thinking about who really was the prime mover, for he thought he knew that already. All he was waiting for was confirmation.

No, the problem which really preoccupied him, which he kept returning to from one direction after another, and one in which he never seemed to make headway, was how to use the information he had to bring the conflict between Copt and Moslem to an end. It had to be soon, it had to be quick, and so far he had seen no way of achieving it.

Not that he had made much progress on anything else. Even Yussuf, the simplest of the problems. He wished he could speak to Zeinab about it. Zeinab was quite good at that sort of thing. Zeinab—oh God, there he went again.

Yussuf. Well, at least *he* had learned his lesson. He would never do that again. He was absolutely ashamed of himself. And as Owen reflected on Yussuf, and on the effects of shame, the glimmerings of an idea began to come to him.

He became aware of someone in the room. It was Nikos.

"He has come back," he said.

"Did he see where Andrus went?"

"Yes."

After the interview Andrus, much to his surprise, had been released; but when he left Mahmoud's office one of Owen's agents had followed on behind him.

"Who did he go to?"

"Sesostris," said Nikos. "As you expected."

"What do you want?" said Andrus.

"I want you to withdraw all your people from the streets, to send them home and to tell them to stay at home, until at least after the Moulid. You are to instruct them not to respond to Moslem provocation. There won't be any after tomorrow, but if there is they are not to respond to it. They are to take special pains not to offend Moslem susceptibilities. Above all, they are not to use any violence. If they do, I expect you to tell me their names and I will deal with them."

Andrus laughed incredulously.

"Is that all you want?" he demanded. "You must be mad."

"It's not quite all," said Owen, "but it will do for a start."

"If you think I'm going to do any of these things," said Andrus, "let alone all of them, you must be crazy."

"I think not."

"Well, I'm not going to do them. Not any of them."

"Oh, but you are."

"If you think you can frighten me," said Andrus, "you are mistaken."

"I don't."

"Then what makes you think I am going to do them?"

"Because if you don't," said Owen, "I shall let it be generally known that Andrus has been giving money to the Moslems for them to use against Copts."

"No one would believe you," said Andrus, but his face went pale.

"Won't they? Even when they hear the evidence?"

"They will believe it to be a trick."

"Even when they hear the evidence? Mordecai?"

"Mordecai would never dare."

"Mordecai has already agreed."

"But—but it wasn't like that."

"Will anyone believe you? Anyone?"

Andrus licked his lips.

"I cannot," he whispered. "I cannot."

"You can," said Owen, "and will."

"Take me to prison."

"No."

"Please."

"If I take you to prison," said Owen, "people will say: 'There goes Andrus, the enemy of the Moslems.' But you are not their enemy. You are their friend. You give money to them to use against Copts. Therefore go free."

Andrus looked at him, stunned. He sat like that for a long time. Then he buried his face in his hands.

"Very well," he said in a choked voice. "Very well. I will do it."

He stood up and almost tottered. He had suddenly aged.

"That is not all," said Owen.

"Not all?"

Andrus seemed totally bewildered. His hands trembled.

"Sit down."

It was as if Andrus's legs had given way under him.

"What more do yo want?" he whispered.

"You are to send a message to Sesostris. You are to tell him that you have to see him urgently. You will tell him that it must be in secret and that it is very, very important. And then you will tell him to come to a place that I will tell you of and at a time that I will tell you. And there you will meet him and say what I tell you."

As realization dawned, Andrus blanched.

"I cannot," he said. "You ask too much."

"Think of this," said Owen, "as payment. Payment for the two men who died because of you and the many who might have died."

"I cannot. I would be ashamed."

"If you do not, the shame will be not just on you but on your father's house. 'There is Andrus,' they will say, 'the man who gave money to the Moslems to use against the Copts.' "

Andrus buried his face in his hands again.

"Either way there is shame," said Owen, "but one way the shame is yours and yours alone. The other way the shame is on your father too."

Andrus sat for a long time. Owen let him sit. When at last Andrus looked up, his face was haggard.

"I will do what you wish," he said.

"What do you want?" said Osman suspiciously.

"I want you to withdraw all your people from the streets, to send them home and to tell them to stay at home. That is, at least until after the Moulid. They are not to let themselves be provoked by the Copts. After today the Copts will be very anxious not to provoke you, but should some foolish man do so then you are to instruct your people not to respond."

"What?" said Osman, unbelieving.

"You are to confine yourself to a mosque until after the Moulid. You will not go out in the streets and you will not say anything in public. There are to be no speeches and no sermons. Not until after the Moulid."

"I shall say what I like and go where I like," said Osman. "As for the Copts, I will cut their throats and dance in their blood."

"You will not," said Owen, who took an equable view of Arab rhetoric.

"No?" said Osman belligerently. "Why won't I?"

"Because if you do," said Owen, "I will tell everyone that you are the man who receives money from Copts."

"I?" said Osman. "I? I receive no money from Copts."

"You go to Mordecai, don't you?"

"He is not a Copt. He is a Jew."

"And where do you think he gets the money from?"

"Not from Copts?" said Osman, with a sinking heart.

"He is just the man in the middle. The Copts bring the money and Osman takes it. Every Friday. On the Sabbath."

Osman reeled.

"Do you swear this?" he said thickly.

"On the Book."

Osman shook his heavy, turbanned head from side to side as if bemused.

"I did not know it came from them!" he muttered. "How was I to know? A man came to me and said there were friends with money. They wished to keep themselves secret and therefore I was to go to Mordecai. But how can they be Copts? Copts would not give money for use against Copts. Unless—"

He smashed his great fists on the table.

"They have tricked me. It was a trap. And I fell into it. Fool that I am!" He buried his head in his arms and rolled about the table in his agony. "Fool! Fool!"

"Osman takes money from Copts. So it will be known."

"Fool! Fool!" groaned Osman. "Oh, the cunning devils! They have beaten me. How shall I show my face? Osman takes Copt money! Oh, the shame of it!"

"If you do as I say," said Owen, "you will be able to show your face. No one will know about it."

"The Copts will tell," groaned Osman.

"They won't," said Owen.

Something in his voice made Osman look at him.

"How do you know?"

"I have talked with them."

"Do not believe them. They are cunning devils."

"On this occasion," said Owen, "I think they may be believed."

"You do not know them like I do," said Osman.

"They have no choice," said Owen. "They are in a trap as deep as yours."

"A trap?" Osman began to sound hopeful. "Of your devising?"

"Yes."

Osman pounded the desk joyfully.

"They are in a trap. The Mamur Zapt has tricked them. They have tricked me but have themselves been tricked."

"That's about it."

"You swear it? On the Book?"

"On the Book."

"Then I will go happily to prison."

"You are not going to prison. You are going to take your people off the streets. Remember?"

"I can't do that," said Osman in consternation.

"You must do it. Or I will see to it that everyone in Cairo knows who is the sheikh who takes money from Copts."

There was a short silence.

"If I do what you ask," said Osman, "can I be sure that the Copts will do the same?"

"You can be sure."

"I do not like it."

"Nor do they."

"No," said Osman, beginning to smile. "Of that one can be confident."

He struck his fist on the table.

"I will do it!" he said.

"At once. Tonight," said Owen.

Osman nodded.

"At once," he agreed. "So it shall be."

He left looking quite pleased. Owen was not sure that whatever lesson Osman had learned had been quite the right one.

Later in the morning Owen paid one of his infrequent visits to the Ministry of Finance. As he was walking along one of the long, green-painted corridors he ran into John Postlethwaite.

"Hello, lad," said John Postlethwaite. "What are you doing here? Come for a bit of pocket money?"

"In a manner of speaking," said Owen. "Not personally, but for the office."

"You'll be lucky. What have you been up to?"

"Not been up to anything. It's all this trouble between Copts and Moslems. It costs money."

"Too true. That's only too true," John Postlethwaite agreed enthusiastically. "That's what I'm always saying. However you look at it, it costs money. These colonies are millstones around our necks, as a noble lord of my acquaintance once said. Mind you, he's a millstone round our necks too, him and all the other lords."

Owen thought that Paul might not like the turn the conversation was taking so hastily shifted tack.

"The real problem is the levy," he said.

"Levy?" said John Postlethwaite sharply. "I've not heard about that."

Owen explained.

"A levy is a mistake," said John Postlethwaite. "It's bad accounting principle. It's a one-off business, you see. You do it once and then that's an end to it. What you want is a charge on something that regularly recurs. You can go on forever then."

"The Khedive's insisting on it. He needs the money."

"What does he need it for?"

Owen thought he hadn't better mention Monte Carlo.

"Oh, a special function he has in mind, I think," he said vaguely.

"If it's an unusual item, then maybe the best thing is a straightforward loan," said John Postlethwaite. "I don't normally approve of loans, unless I'm lending, of course, but sometimes they're the answer."

At the other end of the corridor Owen saw Ramses come out of a door. He began to edge away.

"Come and see us sometime," said John Postlethwaite. "I know Jane would like to see you. She gets a bit cooped up in that hotel."

"Hello," said Ramses. "What are you after? Still in trouble with the Compensation Fund? I might be able to do something for you next year but there's not much chance this year, I'm afraid. We're still stuck in our log-jam."

"Postlethwaite thinks the levy's a bad idea."

"Same here. Unfortunately—"

"He thinks a loan might be better."

"So it might," said Ramses, "if anyone could be found stupid enough to lend to the Khedive."

"I was wondering," said Owen, "if, in return for the levy being abandoned—"

"A loan? You wouldn't get your money back."

"Suppose," said Owen, "somebody made a loan, and the idea of the levy was withdrawn, and Patros became Prime Minister, couldn't he raise taxes?"

"He certainly could and almost certainly will."

"Then the loan could be repaid out of the increase in taxes."

"Why," said Ramses admiringly, "you're beginning to think just like an accountant! Yes, in principle it could be done. I could get a few Copt bankers to club together to find a sufficient sum. It would have to be a loan to the Government, mind, not to the Khedive personally. A special loan so that, say, all the statues in Cairo can be cleaned on time for the Khedive's birthday. They wouldn't be cleaned, of course, but no one would know. A public loan like that would have the added advantage of showing the Khedive what loyal subjects we Copts are and how greatly we admire him."

"You think you could stitch that up?"

"Yes. On condition that the levy were withdrawn. Patros would have to become Prime Minister, too, so that we could be sure that the money would be repaid. Incidentally, I see problems there."

"The Consul-General will agree."

"Yes, but some of our side won't be very happy. As you probably know, there's a strong party among the Copts who are utterly opposed to any Coptic participation in the Government, even on a personal basis."

"As a matter of fact," said Owen, "I think you may find that in future that party is not quite as strong as it has been."

Before leaving the Ministry, Owen rang Paul at the Consul-General's Residency.

"Oh yes," said Paul. "I think that can be managed. I'll have a word with the Old Man. But do you think the Copts will really deliver?"

"I think they will if you can get the Old Man to twist the Khedive's arm enough to persuade him to withdraw the levy."

"OK," said Paul. "I'll see he gets twisting."

Instead of going to the Club as he usually did for lunch, Owen went to Zeinab's apartment. She was surprised and pleased to see him. Afterwards, as she lay drowsily in his arms, she said:

"How is your little Nonconformiste?"

"All right, I think. I haven't seen her since the opera."

"I'm not jealous," Zeinab assured him. "If you want her, you can have her."

"She may have her own views about that."

"Are you taking her to the Moulid?"

"Paul wants me to."

Zeinab was quiet for a moment or two.

"Have you ever been to the Moulid?" she asked.

"Not this one."

"Ah. Then you must take her. Yes, you must certainly take her."

"Perhaps I will," said Owen innocently.

Later, as Zeinab sat brushing her hair, she said:

"How is Yussuf?"

"In the cells."

"Poor man. It is time you let him out."

"I would if I was sure he wouldn't go straight back and do it again."

"He ought to remarry Fatima."

"That's what I'm trying to achieve."

"Have you talked to the man, the one who married her?"

"Suleiman? No. I've talked to Fatima, though. She says that Suleiman will want money."

"Of course."

"Yes, but I haven't any. The Compensation Fund is exhausted. Anyway, it's a bad accounting principle."

"Accounting principle?" said Zeinab, surprised.

"Yes. Give him some and they'll all be doing it."

"That is accounting principle?"

"More or less. Financial control, anyway."

Zeinab shrugged. One of her shoulders emerged from her gown and Owen went across and kissed it.

"I have been thinking," said Zeinab, laying down her brush. "Has Fatima any family?"

"I don't know. I expect so. Why?"

"It is one thing taking a woman into your house," said Zeinab. "It is another thing taking her family."

"So?"

"If she has a large family and some of them are unprovided for, say, for instance, she has unmarried sisters and aunts and nieces, then it is only right, since her husband has married into the family, that he should provide for them, too."

"Yes, but will he see it like that?"

"It is a duty to provide for your wife's family as for your own. Why don't you suggest it to Fatima? She sounds the sort of woman who wouldn't like to let things slip."

"I might do that."

"Yes. If you did," said Zeinab, "you might even find Suleiman ready to think again."

Owen had taken a house in the old part of the city not far from the Mar Girgis. Through the heavy fretwork of its top windows he could see the towering minarets of the Bab es Zuweyla, and from the box window of the storey below, where he was standing when Sesostris approached, he had a good view along the street in both directions.

It was dark and the lamps were lit and they might not have seen Sesostris if he had not had to step aside to avoid a porter with a heavy bundle on his back and stand for a moment in the light from a shopfront. They watched him come to the door.

Owen had had the house cleared and the servant who let Sesostris in was one of his own men. They heard the door close and the footsteps begin to climb the stairs.

In the room Andrus twisted his hands nervously. He was a shell of the man he had been previously. Owen gave him a warning glance. He did not want things to go wrong at this stage.

He glanced round the room to make sure all was in order. It was a modest but comfortably furnished room with a divan, low tables and large leather cushions on the floor. The walls were covered with fine red carpets. Georgiades held one of these aside and stood waiting.

Behind the carpet was a shallow recess in which the bedding was normally stored. When Georgiades and he were standing inside it and the carpet replaced, the wall looked like any other wall.

Sesostris came into the room.

"Well, Andrus?" they heard him say.

"Greetings, Sesostris," Andrus said with difficulty.

"Why have you brought me here?"

"Because it is safest," said Andrus, as they had agreed. "They are watching our houses. My house—and yours."

"Mine?"

"They have found out. The Mamur Zapt knows."

"What does he know? And how do you know that he knows?"

"I have a man in his office. Nikos."

Owen winced. He thought that an unnecessary touch of Georgiades's.

"He has told me."

"How much does the Mamur Zapt know?"

"He knows about the money. And to whom it goes."

"If he knows, why has he not moved?"

"To know is one thing. To be able to prove is another. That is why he is having the houses watched."

"So he is not confident yet. Well, that is useful to know."

Sesostris did not speak for some time. They heard him moving. He seemed to be walking up and down.

"It gives me a chance," they heard him mutter, as much to himself as to Andrus. "The question is whether to stop now or go on."

"I think we should stop, Sesostris," Andrus squeaked uneasily. This part had not been in the script.

"It would be a pity to stop now, just when we are nearly there. A few more days, a week perhaps, would be sufficient. Two weeks at the outside."

"The Mamur Zapt knows."

"But cannot prove. Let us make sure that for the next two weeks he still cannot prove."

"How can we do that?"

"We will not meet. I will get the money to you in some other way."

"That is all right for you," said Andrus with an unexpected flash of his old spirit, "but what about me? He knows I am the organization."

"The church house is watched too?" Sesostris was silent for a moment. "Then you must move somewhere else," he said with decision.

"They will find out."

"But not at once. A week is all we need."

"Is it so close?"

"The Khedive has to decide this week. While there is trouble between Copt and Moslem he cannot offer it to a Copt nor a Copt take it."

"So he will have to offer it to someone other than Patros?"

"Yes."

"That will be a Moslem," said Andrus doubtfully.

"That suits us," said Sesostris with extra definiteness.

"He will impose the levy."

"And that suits us too. It is the only thing that will stir our sleeping brethren, the only thing that will make them fight and not cooperate. It is time," said Sesostris, "to make a stand."

"Yes," said Andrus, with less than his usual certainty.

There was a little silence. Then Sesostris said:

"You are tired, old friend. It has been a hard battle and you have borne the brunt of it. Keep going for just a little longer and then I will have someone else take over."

"I wish you had not given the money to the Moslems."

"It was necessary. They would not have responded on such a scale otherwise. It had to be big, Andrus, for the Khedive to notice and be influenced."

"But for them to use it against our own people!"

"It is hard, I know. But it was necessary. How else are we to break through the effects of centuries of compliance and make the Copts erect and independent once again?"

Again there was a silence. This time it was Andrus who broke it.

"Will there ever be an end to the trouble between Copts and Moslems?" he asked wearily.

"Yes. But on our terms."

"I hope you are right. You play a dangerous game, Sesostris."

The two men talked for a little longer. Andrus was the first to leave. Owen waited, as he had agreed, until the door closed behind him. Then he stepped out from behind the hangings.

CHAPTER 13

The Moulid of the Sheikh el-Herera was peculiar among Moslem saint's days in that its date was fixed not by the Moslem calendar but by the Coptic one. It always fell on Easter Monday. In the view of the Copts this was a deliberate attempt by the Moslems to borrow reflected glory from the greater spiritual event and to obfuscate its uniqueness. In the view of the Moslems the Christian feast was an irrelevance, pursued by the Copts with characteristically unhelpful enthusiasm in order to distract attention from the joyful celebration of the saint's holy day and to clutter up the streets at the time of the Zeffa, or procession, in which the Moulid culminated.

What gave the day added piquancy was that it sometimes coincided, as it did this year, with yet another festival, that of the Sham el-Nessim, the old Egyptian spring festival, elements of which antedated both the Christian celebration and the Moslem one, and which called on the allegiance of all Egyptians whether Christian or Moslem or, indeed, anything else. In practice, the effect of all this was to blur the day into one of general celebration, and tension between Christian and Moslem only erupted into open conflict if things went badly wrong.

At the moment, fortunately, there was no sign of this happening. Everyone seemed in carnival mood. There were children everywhere, many of them dressed up in comic costumes and holding little red lamps. Every so often a few of them would form themselves into a line, each holding on to the coat-tails of the one in front, and then go burrowing through the crowds like snakes to the good-natured protests of the spectators.

The street-artists were out in force. Tumblers, acrobats, dancers, clowns, entertainers, wild men from the south, mixed with spectators and competed for their attention. As the evening wore on and the moment of the procession drew near, they were increasingly joined by small groups of Zikr, dancing and spinning in the light of the lurid, many-coloured lamps with which the streets were festooned.

Musicians were drumming on their tablas and darabukas, flutes were playing and fireworks cracking loudly. As they exploded they lit up for a moment the crowds with their excited faces, startling the donkeys in the donkey-vous and making the little horses stir uneasily. The few policemen on duty gawked heavenwards with the rest.

"It's all quiet, at any rate," said Paul, who had come with them to escort John Postlethwaite or, as he put it, "mark" him.

"Quiet?" said Jane Postlethwaite, her ears still ringing from the last explosion.

"In policing terms, that is," said Paul, laughing. He turned to John Postlethwaite. "I don't know if you were aware, sir, that there's been a bit of trouble lately between the Copts and the Moslems. We were quite worried about that, you know, with Patros Pasha becoming Prime Minister."

"A good man," said John Postlethwaite, "a good financial head on him."

"Yes. Well, in the run-up to the appointment there was quite a lot of tension. It broke out in the occasional incident between Copt and Moslem. Fortunately, Captain Owen has managed to get it under control."

Owen knew that Paul meant to be helpful.

"You'd have your work cut out with this lot," said John Postlethwaite, as a flock of dancing Zikr spiralled down the street holding flaming torches in their mouths, forcing the crowd to swirl and eddy unnervingly. "Religion, I take it."

"What?" said Paul.

On the other side of the street Owen saw McPhee's tall figure. McPhee was there, as he was, partly on purposes of pleasure. They both reckoned there would be no large-scale trouble that night. Small incidents there would certainly be, but both Andrus and Osman had honoured their undertakings and not only pulled their gangs off the streets but instructed them to avoid anything which could lead to trouble.

Across the street McPhee caught sight of them and began to weave his way in their direction.

"Religion's at the bottom of it," said John Postlethwaite. "It usually is."

"Actually, there are a lot of pagan elements too," said McPhee, overhearing and mishearing as he came up, and thinking that Postlethwaite was referring to the festival. "The Sham el-Nessim goes back to pharaonic times and even before, and some of its features, notably the phallic ones, have crept into the Moulid and even into the ceremony of the Coptic Easter."

"A bit of a mixture, eh?" said John Postlethwaite.

"Like Cairo," said Owen; "like Egypt."

In the crowd celebrating the Moslem saint he could see Copts as well as Moslems. The humbler Egyptians saw no incongruity between attending the Christian festival in the morning and the Moslem one in the evening; and the Sham el-Nessim was common to all.

A squeal of pipes in the distance announced the imminence of the procession. The policemen remembered their business and began trying to chivvy people back off the streets, or rather, since that was out of the question, attempting to open up a space through which the procession might pass.

Then round the corner came twelve men bearing aloft cressets full of flaming wood. Behind them came three giant camels draped almost to their feet with a sort of scarlet pall encrusted with shells and bits of brass and mirror. The centre camel had a flat saddle on which stood a Bedouin sheikh in grand robes flourishing a battle-axe. The other two camels carried boys with a kettle-drum slung on each side, which they beat incessantly. Right on their heels were a foot band with more kettle-drums and also cymbals which they clashed and bashed without stopping or having any regard to tune.

Then came the first of the carts, drawn by donkeys and crammed full of children all in gay carnival attire. As they passed, they threw brightly-coloured paper streamers into the crowd.

Other carts followed, each representing some guild of workmen or perhaps just a scene which had struck the organizer's fancy. Around them were masqueraders and tumblers and musicians. The music and the merriment were deafening.

There was a sudden gap in the procession and looks of agitation. The pause became protracted and the crowd fell quiet. And then, struggling round the corner, caught in the lines of lamps and crystal balls which hung across the street, came a huge wooden contraption, a large frame with about fifty lamps on it arranged in four revolving circles, carried by staggering men. Revived by the applause, they struggled on but then were stopped by sudden shouts of alarm. Hanging low over the street in front of them was the shopkeeper's pride, a line hung with huge gilt crystal chandeliers which swung in the wind and made shifting kaleidoscopic patterns of light and shadow. There was a brief halt while eager youths climbed up the shopfronts and hauled the line high enough for the contraption to pass underneath. With a magnificent flourish on the hautboys, the procession resumed.

It took more than an hour to pass. Halfway through there was a friendly touch on Owen's shoulder and somebody produced chairs. The Postlethwaites, unused to the heat, sank into them gratefully.

At intervals the seemingly endless train of carts was broken by items of more direct popular entertainment: troupes of acrobats, jugglers competing against each other, masquerades. Some of the turns were satirical, one of them, for instance, representing a stage Englishman with loud golfing trousers, a Union Jack shirt and a tall top hat, who had the crowd in fits with a continuous stream of what were clearly scurrilous remarks.

"Isn't that a Union Jack?" asked John Postlethwaite.

"I believe it is," said Owen.

"These chaps make use of any material that comes to hand," said Paul.

"Looks a bit of a comic turn to me," said John Postlethwaite.

"Can't quite make it out," said Paul vaguely, who certainly could, and was enjoying it.

Included among the entertainers were various groups of Zikr, which Owen found odd in view of the essentially religious nature of their exercises. The thought came into his mind that Jane Postlethwaite might remark on the fact that for an event ostensibly religious in its inspiration there were singularly few items of specifically religious character, and he hastily pointed out to her that many of the little red and white banners that people were carrying had texts from the Koran inscribed upon them.

"Thank you, Captain Owen," she said politely, and with a certain dryness.

Fortunately, some gorgeous mediaeval palanquins passed at that moment. They were shaped like the cabins of Venetian gondolas and covered with mosaics of silver, ebony and ivory, as rich as the mosaics on an Indian workbox. Each palanquin was slung between two camels, rather peculiarly slung, since the two camels were fastened so close to each other that the head of the rear camel was right under the palanquin, which guaranteed its occupants a boisterous ride.

The front camel was favoured, doubly so, for not only was its head free and erect but it was crowned with a circlet of silver bells and a splendid plume of scarlet feathers.

"The trappings go right back to the Middle Ages, Miss Postlethwaite," said McPhee learnedly. "But then, some of the features of the Zeffa are very odd. They antedate both the Moslem and the Christian eras."

The procession was coming to its climax. The music rose to a new crescendo and along the street came a large cart with a raised platform at the front on which was a royal tableau. "The spring king, possibly," McPhee suggested. The king was a very young king, about fourteen or fifteen years old, though there was no doubt about his being a king since he wore a crown on his head and was richly, if scantily, dressed. Around him were various courtiers, who alternated obeisances to the king with salutes to the crowd.

As the cart approached, they saw that the king was indeed scantily dressed. He was in fact quite naked below the waist. And, attached to his hips by a sort of harness, was a gigantic dildo, grotesquely painted and about two feet long, which waggled and danced in time to the jolting of the cart, to the great delight and applause of all the spectators.

Well, not all.

"I'm a broad-minded chap," said John Postlethwaite,

"but—" He got to his feet. "Come on, Jane. I've had enough. It's time we went."

With a wry glance at Owen, Jane Postlethwaite followed him.

"Boy, do you pick them!" said Paul as he set off in pursuit.

The Postlethwaites returned to England on the following day. John Postlethwaite asserted his influence and managed to secure two cancelled bookings.

"I'll be back," said Jane Postlethwaite.

Fortunately, the end of John Postlethwaite's visit did not entirely efface the otherwise good impressions he had formed during his time in Egypt, and in future he was able to defend the Administration's cause with all the authority of first-hand experience.

The Khedive by then was already in Monte Carlo, obligingly furnished with the resources he needed, and content to leave the management of the realm in the capable hands of his new Prime Minister, who happened to be a Copt.

There was a great deal of pleasure at the new appointment —among the Copts, that was—and Owen was greatly surprised to find that the allocation to the Curbash Compensation Fund rose by a third the following financial year. He was even able to anticipate part of the increase and meet some of his expenses in the current financial year by special arrangement with one of the senior officials in the Ministry of Finance, Ramses.

Sesostris and Andrus both disappeared from the Cairo scene, Andrus for an austere regimen in a Coptic monastery in the desert, where he devoted his time to prayer and fasting, Sesostris for an even more spartan regimen in a less religious but more solid building near Alexandria.

Yussuf remarried Fatima and, much to his surprise after so many barren years, eight months later Fatima gave birth to a baby boy, who, Fatima and Yussuf's sister both swore blind, was the spitting image of Yussuf.

And Owen was able to put to rest Zeinab's fears about the growth of Nonconformist influence in Egypt.

For a time.

About the Author

Michael Pearce grew up in the (then) Anglo-Egyptian Sudan among the political and other tensions he draws on for his books. He returned there later to teach and retains a human-rights interest in the area. In between, his career has followed the standard academic rake's progress from teaching to writing to editing to administration. He finds international politics a pallid imitation of academic ones.